NO WAY OUT

Varida Anthology Volume 1

ISBN: 978-1-937046-38-5

Here we are... trapped in the amber of the moment. There is no why.

Kurt Vonnegut

Prologue

"No Way Out" is more fitting as a title than I realized when I first started collecting these stories. Whether getting past a malfunctioning security bot, escaping a cutthroat, urban nightmare job or facing the possibility of nuclear annihilation; or maybe alien invasion, portals into alternate worlds—expect to be pulled away from your mundane reality into unknown realms. With heroes ranging from the bold and adventurous to the hesitant and unassuming, from human to artificial to ducks. The villains are sometimes thoroughly despicable, sometimes forces of nature, sometimes haunting and unseen. Some are lurking in the implacable inertia of social lunacy. Some are found in their own mind.

Whether you prefer suspense, adventure, intrigue, or humor, there's a little of everything in this collection of science fiction and fantasy stories by Varida P&R authors.

Suzanne Hagelin, January 24, 2024

Table of Contents

Proxy

by Suzanne Hagelin

"Stop." The hand in my face caught me off guard.

"What?" I stammered, breaking out of my absentminded reverie, and focusing on an official looking drone with a badge. It was humanoid from the waist up, bullet shaped from the waist down. It had wheeled up silently in the long, glass-walled passageway and blocked my way. "What's wrong?"

"Identify yourself," it demanded in a flat tinny voice, sunlight glinting off its smooth metal head.

"I am a Pacific Northwest Port Authority official, as you should know," I countered. "What are *your* credentials?" I was accustomed to preferential treatment when traveling, and if security levels were heightened, this statement often got me an immediate pass.

It stared at me for a few moments without lowering its hand.

After three weeks in space attending interplanetary trade negotiations, I was desperate for the tastes and smells of home. Only a few dozen meters away, the exit to wide open spaces beckoned. Fifty meters behind me was the security check I had just cleared. I was alone in the long glassy tunnel, with one bag over my shoulder and a roller at my feet—except for this 1.7-meter-tall bot. Blue skies with wisps of cloud and northern October sunshine arched overhead, framing the hall in cheerful warmth.

"You are not recognized," it informed me.

"I asked you a question," I reminded it, comfortable in my position of relative authority, "and please, lower your hand. I have already come to a standstill and your pose is unnecessary."

The hand dropped to hang at its side. "I am Module KJ-490 point two. I conduct final scans and authorizations of travelers before they exit the restricted zone. This platform has been requisitioned in order to execute my primary function."

"What is your normal platform?" I hated to set my bag down because that would mean I might be detained for more than a few minutes, but the strap was cutting into my shoulder. "Are you saying that your job is to mind the last door at the end of this passage? What are you doing down here?"

"Rephrase the question and provide valid identification," it said, remaining where it was.

"Don't you have access to the security checkpoint I just cleared? I've been identified already!" I was too worn out for this. All I wanted was to get outside, into the sunshine, breathe the free air of my native planet, and go home.

No answer.

"Fine," I muttered, pulling my necklace out of the scarf folds at my throat and unfolding the gold square hinged on it. A glistening, holographic image materialized over it with a bell-like ding and rotated on its axis casting kaleidoscopic colors around. I'm proud of my ID and found myself smiling. The predominance of blue and green said 'home' to me, though it was the encrypted data that would speak to the drone.

"Invalid identification," the unit said flatly, unmoved by the evidence. "It has expired."

"It was valid a few moments ago, at the other end of the hall!" My voice rose a bit in frustration. "Are you telling me it expired in the few seconds it took me to walk this far?"

"The facts are irrefutable."

I stared at it.

It stared back at me.

Taking a deep breath, I folded my ID locket closed and straightened my shoulders. Returning the way I had come to ask for help was no good. It was an exit-only door and there was no one there to ask for help.

"I must exit the passageway," I said, remaining marvelously calm.

"You are unauthorized to exit the Space Port security area."

"I am a citizen of Earth and a resident of this state," I retorted, losing a bit of my calm. "You are committing a crime by detaining me illegally. I submit that your..."

"There is no evidence to support your claims," it interrupted. "You are not authorized to submit any complaints to this unit."

Authorized to make complaints? This was drone-speak for *access*. I understood this, but it annoyed me anyway.

I made a few more attempts to reason with it, but nothing made any difference, so I decided to push past, get out, and deal with the fines later. Picking up my bag, I slung it over my shoulder, grabbed the roller's handle and moved forward, intending to squeeze by on one side.

Drone protocols require that they give way before living people and tame animals. I wasn't in the habit of challenging them, but I had shoved past one or two before. This one was big enough to resist me, however I wasn't easily intimidated.

At least, I never had been before.

The drone's hand snapped out at its side in front of me angled toward the floor. "You will not advance," it said, and with a flick of one finger it cut my arm. Just a graze, nothing serious, but it shocked me.

Turning sideways, I continued to press into the space between the glass wall and the drone, my eyes fixed on the red line oozing on my arm. How had that happened? Was the blasted thing glitching? Miscalculating the distance between my form and its extremities?

Confusion took hold as the drone rolled closer, pressing itself against me, pinning me to the wall. My leg continued to stretch past it as if I could melt by. I was certain it *had* to give way. I was expecting it.

Its arm flexed and it placed its cold, metal hand against my face. With a shove, it knocked me backward, and I landed breathless on the floor. Sitting up slowly, I glanced down at my arm again. The cut was starting to hurt, and the metal hand had left the feel of a cold imprint on my face.

It wheeled toward me, and I found myself scrambling backwards a few paces. Shoving my rolling case with its lower torso, it came to rest at my toes.

"You hurt me!" I jumped to my feet, alarm spreading through me like fire in my veins. This wasn't a security drone with restraint protocols, and besides, no robot could lawfully harm a human being. Fumbling at my ear, I began cell-calling for help, tapping the com-bud repeatedly. "Rogue drone..." I was saying over and over with each tap.

"Unauthorized communications will be blocked," the drone said, rolling a few centimeters closer, now that I was standing and it had room.

"YOU have broken protocol by harming me!" Pointing at its chest with a finger, I mustered courage and grit my teeth, convinced it had been accidental. Surely this would bring about an apology!

"Well within the allowed margin of error," it said, chilling me to the bone. Sunlight glinted on its head and shoulders, flashing in my eyes.

"What margin of error?" I found myself asking, dropping my arm and taking a small step backwards without thinking. "I've never heard of that before."

It rolled forward taking up the ground I had given, placing itself again within a hand's breadth of me. "Yes," it replied. "Now you have."

When the orbit to surface (OTS) shuttle had been descending through the exosphere they had announced that there were some spectacular solar flares hitting the globe at the same time. Most of the planet was well protected and other than some mesmerizing light displays no one earthside would notice. But every now and then, one hears murmurs of malfunctions. An occasional bot that wasn't sufficiently shielded would flip a screw so-to-speak and begin performing erratically. Maybe it was damaged by the solar flare.

What had the robot said? The program inside its chip used to be the exit door module conducting final screenings of the travelers leaving the facility. That would mean it had resided in the chip at the end of this passageway.

And how had it gotten into this drone?

"Listen, KJ," I said, latching onto the only part of its identifier I could remember. "You're malfunctioning. You don't belong in a movable drone. You aren't a robot."

"I open the door for approved travelers. You are not approved and therefore I will not open the door for you. Security has been notified and you will be retrieved."

I found some comfort in that. At least someone was on their way. But I wasn't ready to just give in to the absurdity of it all. "Door?" I challenged, "This isn't a door. This is a drone and you have abandoned your post. The door you're supposed to guard is unguarded." I could see it down there, a glass slider resting in the closed position with detector lights above it. It occurred to me that even if I could squeeze past the bot, I didn't know how to open the door. Of course, someone on the other side might notice me and send help.

"This is the door." The half-witted module thought the bot *was* a door. After a few minutes plotting some crazy debates with it—could I make it think it should be on the other side of me blocking me from the opposite direction?— I realized it didn't have a lot of data to reason with.

It was only a door opener.

"Where is the door?" was the only thing I could think of to say. "Isn't it back there behind you? Look! Go on, turn around and look!" It knocked my arm back as I tried to point at the real exit.

"How long till security gets here?" I peered through the glass walls but couldn't see anything besides trees on one side and a fountain against a wall on the other. There had always been something magical about this little hallway and I had loved it.

Not so much now.

"Security has been notified." The drone rolled uncomfortably close. Why was it doing that? Why did it seem to be encroaching on my space? It was beside my bags now and I realized it was gradually pressing me backwards, centimeter by centimeter. Dropping to one knee I grabbed for my suitcases and yanked them back before the metal hands could stop me. Then I sat down, legs stretched out across the hall as if I were the one blocking the exit. It was the only way I could keep it from shoving me farther back. And it made me feel somewhat less anxious about the whole thing.

"You are violating multiple protocols," I warned, hoping it would feel threatened.

"There is no record of violations," the door-bot corrected me, "You have violated exit procedures and will be taken into custody." The lower half of its body, bullet-shaped with the wide end down, was touching my side.

I wondered if it would begin to shove me and wedged my back against one wall and my feet on the other to resist. Setting my shoulder bag in my lap, I unzipped the main compartment and pulled out a water bottle and what was left of my lunch. It gave me something to do as we waited.

Time dragged itself forward.

A lot of time. Travel delays were a reality I was accustomed to, and I was handling it well. Graciously, in fact. The bottle was soon empty, and the food gone, and the security staff hadn't come yet. Something big must be happening and this little alert just wasn't at the top of the list.

Pulling out a pad, I scanned my email and holo-mail. I read a magazine and reviewed my notes from the meetings I had attended. I did some mild neck and feet stretches. I meditated.

Suddenly it dawned on me that no one else had come through *either* door. No security guards. No travelers. The sun had gone behind some clouds and the afternoon had paled to early evening. No panels lit up to compensate in the passage. It was growing dark, except for the drone's glowing vision-orbs and the distant glimmer from the world at the end of the hall.

"I need a restroom," I informed the drone, rising stiffly to my feet, smoothing out my clothes.

"There are restrooms in the outer lobby," it replied.

"Ok," I dared to hope this was an opening. "Let me go to the lobby restroom."

"Once you have cleared security you will have free access to all the facilities in the lobby," it said cheerfully, turning its head toward me as though it were there to help me.

"Where are those security people? Shouldn't they have been here long ago?" My patience was now threadbare.

"They have been notified," it said, as if there had been no delay.

"What do you do if someone gets stuck in the door?" The idea popped into my head, and I thought it was worth asking. Maybe I could persuade it my life was in danger and it had to let me out.

"Who is stuck?" it asked.

"I AM!" I wanted to argue. I was beginning to get desperate. "I'm pretty sure you aren't supposed to injure me in the fulfilling of your duties. I'm bruised and cut, and I've run out of food and water. I've been sitting here for hours and I'm dying to go the bathroom and I can't because you've detained me *illegally*..." I would've continued with a litany of wrongs along the lines of intimidation and mental abuse, but the drone didn't wait for me to pause.

"Your condition is adequate and waiting for the authorities is the correct procedure."

Something inside me snapped.

"GET... OUT... OF MY... WAY!" I demanded, punching the thing several times in its midsection with the palms of both hands, jolting it back with each blow. It felt good to let my anger loose and assert my rights and let off some steam and...

I went flying backward as it struck back, slamming me with both metallic hands in *my* midsection. My shriek was cut off as I landed and the wind was knocked out of me, something I had never experienced before. It amputated my bravado. "Why?" I groaned once I could stop gasping for air.

The drone rolled forward gaining more space in the hall. "This is for your own protection," it said.

"You mean from you?" I muttered. Home felt farther away than ever, and panic began set in. Had no one thought to find out where I was? Was there no search in motion? Did no one think to check on malfunctioning units? *It's no different than a stalled elevator*, I reassured myself, which was little comfort. Serviceable elevators were so rare these days that people had been known to be stuck in them for days at a time. Well, maybe that had only happened once, but I never forgot it, and I never wanted to be that person.

And it's one thing to be stuck somewhere trying to find a way to get in touch with someone and get help. It's another to be at the mercy of a robot that has the capacity to help but won't.

Jury, judge, jailor, all in one big metal can.

"Check my status again," I tried, curling my legs under me and resting my back against the wall, breathing deeply to calm my racing heart. My bags were now out of reach behind the drone. If I had to spend the night here, it probably wouldn't let me get a sweater or a travel pillow.

"Your identification and security clearance have expired, and security has been notified." The waning light of day made the bot's metallic upper body turn a dull grey, and its lower half faded into a dark charcoal. Its eyes glistened gold.

"When did they expire?" I tipped my head back and stared out the transparent ceiling at the darkening sky.

"Authorization expired at 13:21:19."

"That is literally the moment I walked through the other door, isn't it?" I felt outrage but didn't have it in me to yell. "Hours ago…" This was one of those times when patience was to my advantage anyway. My body ached, and I didn't really want to move.

"Your passage through the first door was authorized." There was a bird flying overhead in the gloom. Must be an owl. The wingspan was huge. Must be hunting.

"Wait a minute…" I scrunched my eyes as I focused on what it had said and mulled it over. "When did you move from your original platform to this one? At what time?"

"Transfer to current location occurred at 13:21:16."

There was something off about that, but I couldn't place why it bothered me. "What instigated the transfer?" I went on, sitting up straighter to stare down at the exit where it belonged.

"The original platform was processing a failure when a cascade of interruptions instigated the emergency alternate protocols. This unit provided a suitable backup."

Now that I thought about it, I had a vague recollection of a robot like this one in the outer lobby waving goodbye as people exited the restricted zone. I had always assumed it was there to answer basic questions like, *Where can I catch a hover taxi?* I suppose it would've had some sort of link to the door mechanism so it would know when a person was exiting.

How bizarre is that? The software governing the door took over a nearby drone and still thought of itself as a security door.

"Your transfer was faulty," I commented. It was unlikely that I could talk it into a dead end, but it was worth a shot. "You neglected to transfer the current traveler authorizations. My security approval got left behind."

"Your assumption is inaccurate. Everything was successfully transferred, and all my systems are intact. I am functioning without flaws."

I never really had been the 'outwit the robot' type.

That's when I realized what must have happened. "You're programmed to update those security markers every thirty seconds or something along those lines, isn't that right?" I said, rising to my feet again, shaking the leg that had gone numb.

"Authorizations are updated every 0.05 seconds."

"Sooo… when was the last time they were updated?" We were face to face now and I was experiencing a sense of elation as if I had cracked a code.

"At precisely 13:21:15."

"You see the problem, don't you?" I smiled in a very friendly way. We could solve this.

"Everything is functioning correctly. There are no problems. Your clearance has expired, and the authorities have been notified."

"Have they? Are you sure they've been notified?" I almost winked. Maybe I could reason with a machine after all.

"Absolutely."

"Have they confirmed that and replied?" I nodded a few times and then dropped my smile, shaking my head as if answering myself. We both knew they hadn't.

No answer.

"No one is coming, KJ," I glared at it. "You aren't connected to the system anymore. It's been fried, can't you tell? Can't you detect the missing connection?"

"There is a gap at this time. Waiting for reconnection is the correct response. I am expecting a reply."

For a moment I thought I might weep, but I didn't. I found I still had some self-control left and I might've been a little dehydrated.

"How long, KJ? HOW LONG?" I yelled, squeezing my eyes shut; they were really dry. And my bladder was painfully over full. "Don't you understand that you've been disconnected for a long time and that your decision to detain me is WRONG?!"

"Updates are established every 0.05 seconds," it replied absurdly.

"So basically, you're telling me that you don't even keep track of how long it's been since your last update. That's what you're saying, isn't it? As far as you know… wait…" I looked up through the glassy roof with a groan. "How much are you retaining of our interactions? What's the first thing you remember about me?"

"My first recording of you is when you came through the security door at the end of the hall."

"And you remember looking at my ID?"

"It is expired. You have no valid identification and the authorities…"

"Yeah, I know, the authorities have been notified." The hall had grown quite chilly, and the cold was seeping into my body. And my situation was becoming desperate. If I didn't find a way out, I wouldn't be able to prevent the humiliation of being detained without basic facilities, and by that, I mean, a viable toilet. Flashes from early childhood burst into my mind and I began drumming my feet on the floor.

"You are moving at zero kilometers per hour," it observed helpfully.

"Can't you see?" I pleaded, "I have got to find a bathroom. You've kept me in here for several hours and this is outside of all AI parameters! You CAN'T treat me this way! You'll be dismantled when I get out—if I ever get out of here…PLEASE!"

"All parameters are in place. Your observations are meaningless."

It was too stupid to have even a basic AI human-care module.

It was just a subroutine.

Something about that cut through my impervious, self-focused bubble. All my annoyance and exhaustion melted away as I looked at it and considered that it was doing the best it could with what it had. Part of my mind mocked the idea, the other part... It wasn't anything approaching human—but something about it touched the human side of me. I had been injured once and unable to think clearly or function properly. It had taken a long time to recover. And I knew other people who had been permanently damaged or were born with limitations that required they handle daily life very differently from most people.

I remember what it means to be broken… and to need compassion.

The passageway was very dark at this point, the drone's visual panel being the only source of light. I saw it now as hollow; it was a cavernous metal chassis filled with empty spaces; capable of riches, roomy enough for the most sophisticated programs. All it had was a door-opener app.

For a moment I identified with it, and imagined wanting to have more purpose, wanting to experience more life, to acquire and ponder knowledge, to explore. I wished for it that it could expand.

I forgot that it was a misplaced door.

Reaching up, I fumbled at my throat, then wrapped my arms around its neck. It bore the embrace wordlessly, colorlessly. As I let go, it rolled back and to the side, leaving a wide gap. I didn't hesitate and never questioned the wisdom of moving past. It didn't even occur to me that it might knock me down again.

I sailed past the door-bot, picked up my bags, and ran down the hall to the final glass door which slid open of its own accord.

For years now since then, people have talked of the strange drone in the northeast lobby of the Walla Walla spaceport. It's become something of a mascot, loved by locals, sought out by travelers. It likes to stand at the window looking out or wheel around the lobby with its head turning from side to side, as if smiling, nodding, and sometimes waving to the people it passes. Sometimes it stands at the exit threshold, just on the verge of the outdoors, gazing out into the fresh air, soaking up sunshine. Articles have been written about it and there's no end to the video clips taken of it.

I've often wondered why no one tried to decommission it—I suspect they were charmed. It hardly ever speaks but when it does, there are only a few words that come out. "I am a citizen of Earth and a resident of this state," is its most popular saying. And I think this must have been the one that gained it a privileged status.

Around its neck hangs a chain with a gold square locket. Every now and then, it comes to a standstill in some arbitrary place, opens it, and stares at the glimmering, rotating image flickering with blue and green. After a few moments, it puts it away again.

Sometimes it makes me chuckle when I think of it. I had given it my ID on impulse, as if I could win it over as a friend. There was no clear thought on my part. Just an instinctive gesture of kindness. I never expected it to make such an impact.

And clearly, it has found a way to enjoy the environs it inhabits as it waits for a security clearance that will never come.

The drone believes it is me.

"Proxy" was first published in the Northwest Independent Writer's Association 2020 Anthology.

The Watcher in the Wood

by Nia Jean

I fled through the trees, lungs screaming for more air than I could suck in. For all I knew the mountain lion was on my heels, mere seconds from putting an end to my life. There was no time to catch my breath, and so I ran without stopping, one hand pressed to my ribcage. Painful twinges spiked through my nerves with every step.

It was foolish of me to go camping alone, what was I thinking? The North Cascades National Park was beautiful, especially in early fall, but I was close to the border of Canada and far past the designated camping areas. There were rules about where one could and couldn't camp, warnings about wild animals, but I had heeded none of them. Whether it was subconscious or not, I assumed that nothing like that could or would happen to me. So, when I left my tent to fill my water bottle and saw the mountain lion standing by the creek's edge, I was shaken. It turned its head, not even spooked at the sound of my approach, and made eye contact with me. Then I ran without looking back.

This is only what I deserve, I thought. *I have no one to blame but myself.* Where I was going, I didn't know, hopefully back toward my tent or the safety of the campgrounds. Instead, I found myself sprinting deeper into the midst of the trees, their long trunks towering over me like giants. Nothing looked familiar. The forest deepened and became more overgrown, the ground covered in large ferns and plentiful mushrooms. I ran through the underbrush leaving it trampled and disturbed behind me.

Ahead of me two trees, dead and covered in moss and flowery weeds, leaned toward one another with their branches almost woven together like a canopy. If I had not been running for my life, I would have stopped to take a picture. Instead, I ran through it, fearing that my death was right behind me.

My legs gave out not long after, throwing me forward onto the earthy ground. Rolling onto my back, I choked in breaths of air like a fish out of water, eyes wildly darting to and fro around me. Where was the lion? Surely, I couldn't have lost it that easily.

All I could hear was my own heartbeat pounding in my ears, and tiny specks of light danced in front of my eyes. *I'm passing out,* I thought in despair, imagining the lion just beyond my realm of vision, stalking me with merciless hunger. My heart turned toward the blue sky, lifting a silent plea for help before consciousness was stolen away from me by exhaustion.

The smell of a wood fire roused me, and I found myself waking up with a thick fur laying on top of me. Bewildered, I lay there wondering what dream I had entered, or if this in fact was real and my frantic escape had been the dream. I sat up and looked around, unsure how much time had passed. Where was I?

A simple campsite greeted my eyes. There was a minimal fire set into a shallow hole dug into the earth, surrounded by a circle of rocks. To my left a figure clothed in leathers and hooded by a gray-green cape was busy pitching a tent made of canvas. Hearing my movement, the figure turned from what he was doing and observed me from the cover of his hood. I could only see the lower half of his face—a stubble-covered jaw with a thin mouth pressed together thoughtfully—but something about him made me feel safe. My first thought was that he must be a park ranger, but his attire wasn't right.

"Are you alright?" he asked, his voice gentle as though he were speaking to a frightened animal instead of a person.

I looked around me for any sign of danger and found none. We were alone in the woods, the only sound the warm crackling of flames on dry wood. "I think so," I said.

"I'm glad," he smiled. He went back to his tent, pulling its ropes tight and hammering wooden pegs into the earth. "I've almost got the camp set up, so I am glad you are awake. There's food cooking, it should be done presently."

My eyes shifted toward the fire, though I could see no pot or grill over it. What food was he referring to? "Thanks," I said, and my stomach grumbled in agreement. "So... who are you?" I didn't know where he had come from, or why he was dressed the way he was. *Maybe he's part of a renaissance fair. Or worse, what if he's one of those role-playing types?*

He did not respond at first, finishing his tent before taking a seat beside the fire. "My name is Alen," he remarked. "You have nothing to fear from me, I am not one of them."

I frowned. "Them?" I asked carefully. I had no idea what he was talking about.

"The ones you were running from," he said.

"I was running from a lion," I said, looking nervously over my shoulder. I couldn't tell from which direction I had come. There were giant evergreens as far as the eye could see, and they all looked the same to me.

"Ah," he nodded, letting his hood fall back against his shoulders to reveal a kind-looking face with narrow eyes beneath thick eyebrows. His rough-shaven face was framed by dark brown hair he kept tied behind him in a simple braid, not long enough to reach past his shoulders. "Then you are lucky indeed. This forest is dangerous, very few who enter leave here alive."

Well, that was reassuring.

"Look," I began, "I know I was supposed to stick to the campgrounds, I'm sorry. I won't do it again! Thank you for helping me escape that mountain lion, but can you please bring me back to the entrance now? I just want to go home." I didn't want to be out here with a role-playing stranger any longer than I needed to be, even if he did seem like a decent person.

The man watched me in confusion, eyebrows furrowed together. "What?" he asked, as if nothing I had said made sense.

I was starting to get annoyed. "I'm sure your *role* is important, but it has nothing to do with me," I said, raising my voice sharply. "I wanna go home!"

"Where is home?" he hesitated, a somewhat anxious expression on his face, as though he didn't know what to do with me.

I was done playing this game. "Seattle," I said, though it wasn't entirely true. I was from a smaller suburb a couple hours north of it. "Look, Alen or whoever you are, this isn't funny."

Alen offered me a smile, attempting to reassure me. "I don't know this 'Seattle' place, but the edge of the forest isn't far. I can guide you there if you like. We should probably wait until morning, it's not wise to travel the forest at night."

I drew my knees to my chest, shivering at the chill air around us. With the sun now sinking below the horizon, there wasn't much warmth left in the silent woods, and I knew that he was right. Trying to set off on a hike after dark was foolish. My experience with the mountain lion had taught me that. "Okay," I relented. "I'm sorry, I'm just scared."

He looked relieved and returned to stoking the fire. "I understand," he said. "Duskers are dauntless hunters, you're lucky to have escaped. They don't easily let their prey get away from them..." He looked at me expectantly, waiting for me to give him my name.

"Becca," I supplied.

Alen smiled warmly. "Nice to meet you, Becca."

I nodded, and wrapped one of his furs around me, staring at the fire between us in silence for several moments. "What's a dusker?" I asked.

"Forest lions. They often come out at dusk to hunt, which is why we call them duskers. Why, what do you call them?"

"Mountain Lions," I shrugged. "Or I guess we call them pumas, too."

"Pumas?" he chuckled. "I haven't heard that one."

"Don't they call them pumas where you live?"

"Not that I've heard," he shook his head. "Seattle must be a very different place from here. Is it a large country?"

I gave him a look, not amused. "It's a city," I said. "And I guess you could say that it's big. Traffic is pretty bad." It was rated one of the worst in the country for commutes, if I remembered exactly, but it was nowhere near New York City size. "Where are you from?" *Canada?* I wanted to add but didn't. He didn't have an accent, but there was something different about the way he spoke that felt foreign to me.

"I live here," he gestured around him. "The Timberland has always been my home."

Definitely Canada, I thought to myself with a nod. Maybe he doesn't even know he's over the border? Or maybe he's here illegally. Though I wasn't about to bring that up in conversation.

He caught my expression and misunderstood it. "Don't worry, Becca," he reassured. "We'll be able to reach the forest's edge in just a few days if we make good time."

I looked up in alarm at this comment, my heart beginning to race. "A few days?" I blurted. "What are you talking about? It's only a few hours hike from the campgrounds, I came out here only just today!"

"That can't be," Alen's brows knit together in an expression of suspicion. "The nearest city is four days by foot, you couldn't have gotten here in one day."

"Well, I DID!" I yelled.

At that moment I was painfully aware of how still the forest was. The silence felt treacherous, like a thin layer of ice atop a vast depth of water about to crack beneath my feet.

Alen scowled and peered into the dusk, one hand rested on the hilt of a blade strapped to his belt that I had not noticed until this moment, and the sight of it did not reassure me in the slightest. "Quiet," he said softly. "It's not wise to raise your voice in the territory of the Watcher."

I wanted to ask him what the Watcher was, but I couldn't find my voice. There was a heaviness in the air, an invisible pressure that made every hair on my body stand on end, and I knew instinctively it was the feeling of imminent danger.

Eventually he relaxed and turned to face me once more. "I don't know where you came from, or how you managed to get here. But you are here now, and if you want to survive the trip home, you'd do well to keep your voice lowered and your wits sharp. We are not alone in these woods."

I got the distinct impression he was not referring to duskers. "So, you're saying," I said, my voice much quieter, though I pronounced each word with a sharp staccato, "we are *not* in the National Park?"

He reached his stick into the fire, rolling two blackened oblong lumps out of the coals. "I don't know of any place by that name," he said gravely.

"And I suppose you've never heard of Seattle either," I scoffed.

"There are many cities I know nothing about. I've lived here all of my life, and rarely step foot out of the wood."

"And these Watchers, are you sure they aren't just Park Rangers you're trying not to get caught by?"

Alen didn't seem to know how to reply to this. He studied me for several moments, carefully rolling the objects he'd pulled from the fire into wooden bowls. "I wasn't following you," he finally said.

I didn't know what that had to do with what I asked, but I just rolled my eyes and dropped the subject. I didn't believe him, nor was I going to go along with whatever game he was playing. If he kept me safe from the mountain lions, I would put up with the charade, but that didn't mean I would be happy about it. *One thing's for sure,* I thought. *I never want to go camping again.*

We didn't speak to each other much after that. After a while, he handed me one of the wooden bowls with what seemed like a baked yam--one of the black things he pulled from the fire--and told me to cut it open and eat the inside. I was grateful for the food, and even though it desperately needed salt, it was warm and filling and even a little sweet. I didn't remember yams tasting quite that good. When we had finished eating, we threw the charred skins into the fire, and he gestured toward the tent with a nod. "I'll keep watch," he said.

The comment didn't encourage me, but the tent was warm, and I curled up under the furs with minimal discomfort. I thought I would stay awake like that forever, worrying endlessly about the stranger sitting just outside, the danger of mountain lions, and the invisible Watcher in the woods. But before I knew it, I had slipped quietly into a deep and dreamless sleep.

‡—‡

I was sluggish the next morning, and I did my best to help Alen roll up the furs and take down the tent. When we finished tearing down, he began to pack everything into a very weathered hiking pack that looked well past its prime.

"Ever heard of REI?" I chuckled when I saw it. He was in a serious need of some upgraded equipment if he planned on being out here camping all the time.

He looked at me curiously. "I haven't," he said. "Who is she?"

I blinked, hesitating to reply until I decided he really had no idea what I was talking about. "It's a store," I said. "You know, with camping and hiking gear? You've really never heard of it?"

"I don't really enter cities," he said, looking uncomfortable. He shouldered his pack and cleared his throat. "We should get started right away, but The Ancient Arch is not far. We can stop there to eat something if we're quiet."

"Sure," I replied indifferently. I was relieved that he wasn't making me carry anything for the walk. "What's the Ancient Arch?"

He led the way through the trees, and I followed a few paces behind him. "It was once a great doorway," he explained. "Now it is merely a broken remnant of a time long past. I never learned much of its history, but it's one of the landmarks of the forest."

I wondered if it was the same natural archway I had run through the night before, and it reassured me. It meant we were going the right way. "I don't remember it being very far, but who knows?" I murmured to myself. The fantasy game he was insisting on playing annoyed me, so I was doing my best to ignore it. As long as we made it back, I didn't care.

The walk was easy as the ground was fairly level, broken only by trees, roots, ferns and fallen branches. Occasionally the trunk of a dead evergreen would be lying in our way, and we would be forced to climb over it or go around it. On and on we walked in what seemed to me no particular direction. Everywhere I looked there was more of the same, a never-ending labyrinth of trees that seemed identical to my eyes.

It was almost an hour before we reached the edge of a small clearing, where he stopped and turned to face me with a proud smile. "Here we are," he said, stretching his hand out toward the center of the open glade. "This is the Ancient Arch. Incredible, isn't it?"

Before us stood a large stone archway, blanched white by the sun. On either side of it two trees grew up so close they were nearly a part of the stone columns themselves. They were not evergreens, in fact they looked more like maple trees by their branches, though both of them were long dead. Moss clung to their bark and to the white stones like a carpet, and intricate purple flowers dotted the lush green. I had never seen anything like it before, and yet it seemed familiar to me. Since when were there ruins in the park like this?

I walked toward it, unnerved by the sight. "This can't be the same arch," I said, beginning to circle it to see the other side. When I reached it, I froze in place, my throat tightening in fear. They were exactly the same as the two trees I had run through last night, except for one thing. There was a path of white stone steps leading up to it that I was certain had not been there previously.

"Look," Alen remarked. I tore my eyes away from the leaning trees and saw that he was crouched on the ground on the opposite side. "Someone has been here recently. See these footsteps? They must have been in a hurry."

I walked toward him, peering down at the disturbed earth, but before I had a chance to say anything, he reached out to pick something up from the ground. He held it up curiously, turning it over in his hands with a bewildered expression, and immediately I snatched it away from him. "My phone!" I exclaimed. Why hadn't I thought to search for it before now?

Alen glanced between me and the archway, his eyes widening. "Becca," he said slowly. "Did you say you came through some trees like this when you were fleeing the dusk—the puma?" he corrected himself at the last second, and by his tone I felt like it was significant somehow.

"Yes," I said, trying to turn on my phone. It was dead and would not respond. "At least I think so. But this can't be the same one, it doesn't look right." Yet I couldn't deny that this was my phone. I felt the hairs on my neck begin to stand on end, disliking the eerie feeling growing in my stomach.

Alen stood, backing up a step. "Do you know what the Ancient Arch was supposed to do?" he asked, though it was clear by his tone he already knew my answer. He continued, hesitating only slightly. "It was a doorway. They say that it was used to travel great distances, even to other worlds."

I was afraid now. I wanted to believe that this was just a game, to be angry at him for including me in the charade without my permission, but I couldn't shake the feeling that something wasn't right. "I've had just about enough of this," I blurted. "I'm tired of the fantasy games, okay? I just want to go home."

"I don't think that's possible," Alen said, and his expression was grave. "This door is closed, and has been for hundreds of years, perhaps even thousands."

"Stop it!" I screamed. I wouldn't believe him. I couldn't. When I spoke again, it was with much more restraint. "Stop playing games."

"Becca..." he started toward me, then halted. His face turned hard, and in a flash, he drew his blade and held it out before him, eyes fixed on something over my shoulder. The

24

bronzed blade was deathly cold in a way that I couldn't describe, as though I could sense it more than see it with my eyes. "Get behind me," Alen ordered.

I whirled around instead. What I saw seemed unreal, and for a moment all I could do was stare. Then I laughed, though to me it almost felt like a sob that had gotten stuck in my throat. *I must be dreaming,* I reasoned.

At the edge of the clearing stood what I thought was a person on four legs, but a second look revealed a person-sized insect not unlike a praying mantis. It was green in color, with a sectioned abdomen and eyes on either side of its head, and two antennae twitching side to side as it observed us. Where a praying mantis would have two large sickle-like arms, this creature had four, and each arm sprouted three knife-like fingers, outstretched as though to grab at me. On its face was a sharp beak for a mouth, clicking as it rubbed together.

This was not something that existed in real life. This was the stuff of nightmares.

Before the insect could move, I felt Alen grab my arm and yank me backwards. I stumbled and fell to the ground, landing hard on the stone steps behind me. It hurt. "Stay back, Watcher!" he uttered sharply, stepping in front of me with his chilling sword before him.

Clicking and hissing at us, the insect skittered forward slowly, its large eyes fixed on me. It moved first to one side, then the other, letting out a sharp angry hiss as Alen followed its movements staying between it and me. Arms twitching in fury, it bent down on its digitigrade legs and sprang forward at me.

With a swipe of his blade, Alen severed two of its arms, then kicked the creature back before it could reach me. It landed several feet back, beak clicking together in a sharp snap, before it twisted around and launched at me again with incredible speed, almost like the grasshoppers I used to catch in my grandparents' backyard.

Alen was ready, planting himself between me and the bug, and ducking out of the reach of the insect's claw-like fingers. He made another swift jab with his sword, but this time it met with air as the creature avoided the strike. I couldn't keep up with their rapid movements. The cold sword slicing through the air left gusts of chill wind in its wake. A torrent of jabs and blows from the alien arms were so rapid they blended in my vision. I watched helplessly, numb at the idea that I might lose the one person who could help me get home. All I could do was sit there with my mouth open in horror.

Just as it seemed that Alen might lose, the creature leapt straight at him. At that moment, Alen twisted his hands and brought his sword upward from below with a loud yell. The blade separated the insect's head from its body, and it fell to the ground with a dying hiss, wounds seared closed by ice.

I lay upon on the stone steps with my body rigid, struggling to breathe. I could smell the creature's astringent blood, hear its flesh sizzling from the burning ice wounds, and at the back of my mind, an unsettling thought began to surface. What if this was no dream? What if… it were real?

Several seconds later I realized Alen was calling my name. I looked up, meeting his eyes, and found that I could breathe again.

"That was a Watcher," he said grimly. Even though his clothes were torn and there was blood on his face and shoulder, he reached down and offered me his hand. I took it, and his grip was firm as he pulled me to my feet. He did not let go till he was sure that I was steady. "There can be no denying now what happened."

"What *did* happen?" I asked. My voice felt distant, as my brain tried to catch up with what I had just witnessed. I couldn't believe that any of this was real, but how could I deny what I had just experienced? The doubt in my mind sent a shiver of dread down my spine.

And what do I do if it is real? Am I stuck here, forever? What if all this is just purgatory, and I'm already dead? My legs felt weak, and I nearly let myself fall down to the ground again.

Alen's face was patient as he looked at me, and he began to clean his blade, being careful not to touch it, before returning it to its sheath. "Don't you see? This doorway behind you..." he said. "You must have come through it from your world, there's no other reason they would seek you out and try to kill you."

"But what *are* they? Why would they want to kill me? It's not my fault I ended up here!" Even as the words tumbled out of my mouth defensively, I felt guilty for saying them. It *was* my fault. I went into an area I wasn't allowed to go, a place that I was warned was dangerous. In a way, I *did* deserve whatever consequences came from my stupidity, though now all I could think about was how I would never be so foolish again, if only I were just given the chance to get home. *I'll do anything, please, just don't let this be real!*

"They are the Watchers. It's said that they came from the Doorways too, once upon a time." Alen began to pace back and forth between the dead Watcher and the broken archway as he spoke, staring downward at the trodden earth. "It's said that they guard them jealously, allowing no one to pass through. This one is closed, so I had assumed they wouldn't be here. But then..." he looked at me with an incredulous expression. "You came through."

"I'm sorry," I whispered. *I want to go home. I want to see my family again.* My feelings of longing and regret were so strong, I burst into tears.

Alen came toward me, his expression awkward as he gave me an encouraging pat on the shoulder. He was quiet for a moment, watching me sob with his eyebrows furrowed in thought. "It's not going to be easy for you here, I can see that," he said quietly. "You'll need to learn how to defend yourself if you want to survive any more encounters with the Watchers."

Choking back my tears, I looked at him with unadulterated frustration. "Is that supposed to be encouraging?" I demanded. The last thing I wanted was to see another one of those things!

Almost as if I hadn't spoken, he kept going. "The nearest city is not far, at least. I don't know if you have anything of value to trade, but I am sure we could find you what you need there."

"What's the point?" I exclaimed miserably. "I don't know the first thing about this place, how am I supposed to get by when there are *monsters* out there? My phone doesn't work, I don't have any of my things, and that broken pile of rubble—" I turned and pointed accusingly at the dead archway behind me, "—was my only way home!"

Alen flinched, as though my words caused him pain. He stood in front of me in silence, his eyes not meeting my face. "That's not entirely true," he said at length.

I wiped tears and dirt from my face with my sleeve. "Right," I muttered unhappily. "There's more of these useless ruins out there, all guarded by angry nightmare bugs. Anything else I'm leaving out?"

"I could teach you," he said. His voice was so quiet I barely heard him. "If you want me to. How to fight, to travel, to hide from them."

The offer didn't exactly make me feel hopeful. "What's the point?" I asked again. "No matter what I do, it doesn't change the fact that I'm stuck here. I don't ever want to see one those things again!"

"Neither do I," Alen snapped, frustration rising in his voice. "But you're not going to make it without my protection!" He took a deep breath and added more calmly, "I'm willing… if you want me to."

I took an unsteady breath and let it out slowly. "I do want your help."

My words brought a faint smile to his lips. "I will teach you what you need to know in order to live here," he promised.

No matter how hard I tried, I could not keep my tears from spilling down my cheeks. *I don't want to live here,* I thought unhappily. *I want to go home.* But all I said was "okay."

He helped me to my feet and led the way through the trees, picking up his belongings as we passed by the body of the Watcher. I stopped to give it one last scathing glare before plodding after him. "How long did you say it would take to get to the city?" I asked hopefully.

"Only a few days," Alen replied. He looked up at the sky in thought. "Then we'll need a few days to get more provisions. The journey might take several weeks."

"What journey?" I refrained from groaning, dreading any more time spent in the wilderness. "Do we have to go tromping through the woods to avoid the Watchers? Why can't we just stay in the city?"

He turned and looked over his shoulder at me, bewildered. "Don't you want to go home?" he asked.

I just stared at him with my mouth open as I tried to figure out what to say. Of *course,* I wanted to go home! "Didn't you say the doorway is closed?" I demanded.

That same look of frustration crossed his face. "*That* doorway, yes." He glanced past me through the trees, his eyes fixed on the ruin. "But I know where to find another."

All at once, I understood his hesitation, the need for provisions, and his admonition that I would have to learn to survive.

Our eyes met and hope surged inside my chest.

There was another door.

And Alen was going to take me there.

"The Watcher in the Wood" was first published in the Northwest Independent Writers Association 2019 Anthology.

Parallel Mother

Trembling with anguish, I embrace my son, the cyberwolf expiring at my feet. He clings, but only one can use the portal. The willow rustles as he fades and I collapse, the headline changing. "Missing Boy Found," it says now.
But not for me.
She, not I, will raise him.

A 50-word sci-fi mystery first published on Medium in WEPAW Bloggers, March 2023.

The Lost Forest

by Eric Little

Nico liked to have tea and a chocolate croissant every morning before work at the Café Argos. The small café was run by Farid and his wife Carmen, who always brought him his usual fare without waiting for an order. They were very polite and a little nervous in dealing with him because of his status. He wanted to smile and tell them to relax, they didn't need to be afraid of him—but he never did.

He wore a mask every day of his life.

This morning, their young daughter Soli was serving pretend tea to her doll by the counter, but Carmen swept her up and bustled her to the back when she saw Nico watching her. He understood; the mega-city was a dangerous place for the powerless, and they were just protecting their child. He left a larger tip than usual when he finished and pretended not to notice the obsequious thanks Farid showered on him.

The office was only a ten-minute walk from the café, and Nico's long legs took him there quickly. He wondered, as he often did, how many of the people he passed were pretending to be someone else. Being constantly surrounded by psychopathic bosses encouraged a cynical mind-set. But maybe there really were others like him out there, hiding in plain sight. He sighed. Maybe even love was possible, someday... Nico was, if nothing else, a pre-Raphaelite romantic at heart. He hid that too.

As he crossed the Office Commons, he noticed workers mopping up something and carting away a few broken desks, so he smoothly detoured around and continued his journey without a pause. The bureaucrats of the Commons are territorial but almost always backed down from middle-management executives such as Nico. The higher your position, the deadlier you were to cross. Even the crazies rarely messed with Nico. Just because he avoided fighting didn't mean he was unskilled at combat: when you swim with sharks, you need to have a fearsome bite.

Nico's lanky body relaxed a bit as the security doors into his office enclave slammed shut behind him, and he made his way to his personal office. Collapsing into his form-molding chair, he willed his heart to slow its beating. The incident with the little girl at the café had rattled him and crossing the Office Commons can be a precarious journey when you're your mask isn't on straight. No one noticed, he decided, or I'd be dead by now.

Nico's greatest fear was to be revealed for the gentle soul he was. Then he would be everybody's meat.

In the Corp-cities everyone works for the company. Competition for advancement was cutthroat, especially down in the trenches of the Office Commons. Nico spent his days surrounded by sociopathic middle-managers, most of whom lacked the kind of restraints that empathy brings to the table. In the mega-city Seacouver, sometimes the boss really is out to get you!

All he was sure of was that if he was found out, he'd quickly find himself transferred to the Waste Management Division.

Nico started going over the morning's numbers and returning messages. An hour later he rose and made his way to the boss's office bunker for the usual Tuesday manager meeting. As he did his thoughts wandered to his secret passion.

It had all started with a book.

Nico found it when he was ten. Its beautiful colored pages were faded and a few torn, but it was the words that blazed in his mind like a fire. The book was called "Paradise Lost" and told the legend of a lost forest. He had never heard of a forest before, but the illustrations were beautiful, and oddly familiar. It looked like... a home he had never known.

He had read it over and over until he no longer needed the book to see the words and images in his mind. "...a real, living Pacific Northwest forest, with soaring Hemlock and Red Cedar and Firs as far as the eye can see. Beneath their majestic branches a frilly two-meter-high fern sea sways in the lilting woodwinds. Slicing the ferns are numerous streams ripe with fat trout and salmon, just waiting to be caught and eaten. There are shadowy mushroom caves next to meadows of waving barley. It is a lost paradise hidden behind an amber door..."

And it couldn't be farther from his real life.

Nico's promotion to middle management had brought him status and a new measure of freedom. At last, he had some influence over the bullies, and reduced oversight allowed him to pursue his greatest desire: finding the long-lost Door to Paradise. He constantly daydreamed of escaping the mega-city and living a quiet life in the forest, if he could just find the right exit.

Nico successfully hid it, but most of the time he was just plain scared. You'd think that growing up among the hyena gangs and political packs, he'd be hardened by now. That the day-after-day brutality would have numbed his soul to the pain of others, but no; he still felt every blow and death as if it were himself being punished.

He was bone-weary of the suffering management reveled in. He was tired of pretending to be one of the monsters, all the while lugging a huge fear-tumor that only he could see.

Nico swallowed as he approached the boss's conference room and politely 'knocked' by implant two minutes before the meeting was to begin. The fortified office doorway slid open noiselessly and Nico walked in at a casual pace. When he passed the boss's trophy wall, he pretended to admire the innocent but terrible things he saw. Today, there was something new, an antique pocket watch. Funny, the boss's rival had owned one just like it! Luckily, Nico's mask let none of his thoughts show. Everyone knew the boss was in the habit of watching as they came in to make sure his managers were impressed with his newest addition.

They always were.

Nico observed one of the newer managers stroke the boss's ego by complimenting his newest trophy. He was quite capable of kissing butt too; when you have to pretend to be something you aren't, such skills develop quickly. But he limited his compliments to two a week. Only amateurs fawned daily. Drop to less than two and the boss gets to wondering if you're part of the team.

The boss liked to start the meeting with their weekly numbers, and then dissect the problem areas afterword. This way he could watch them sweat as they waited for the "course correction" that was coming their way. Nico was very observant as a matter of survival, and noticed the Renee was a little pale. She was also quietly carrying on a frantic conversation with someone by implant. Then the meeting started.

Nico turned his primary attention to the boss. His figures showed modest growth this week and didn't require any corrections. Nico hid his relief; it was short-lived anyway.

The boss began chewing on the latest unlucky employee, Renee, who trembled minutely and was white as a ghost by now. The other managers sensed blood in the water and leaned forward to get a better view.

"It seems that some of my $creds have vanished while you were in possession of them. What kinda inept excuse are you going to trot out to distract us from your greediness?" demanded the boss. Everyone leaned forward a little more at the word "us".

If only Nico had known ahead of time! If Renee had come to him—but now there wasn't enough time now to help cover up the discrepancy. The boss abruptly stood, stretched, and began to meander closer to her, almost as if by accident, as he continued gnawing on the unlucky subordinate. Nobody was fooled by this, especially not Renee. You could see too much white in her eyes as she began babbling her excuses.

Nico hated the hunt.

"...almost have proof that the Claims department is behind this, if I just had a little more time to..." Renee was saying. Then she gasped as the boss seized her by the back of the neck, lifted her out of her seat, and passed her to the security team that had suddenly materialized. They disappeared with the luckless Renee just as fast. Her hazel eyes met Nico's as she was dragged out the door, and he felt loss, even if he didn't really know her very well. The boss slid back into his seat, languidly cracked his neck, and looked over his team, a satisfied smile on his face.

"Renee is being transferred. Post a job opening in Supplies," he ordered the Human Resources manager. Nico caught a smug look flashing over the Claims manager's face—she was obviously behind the whole thing.

"Send my tactical accounting team to her apartment," he added, sending the amateur who had fawned over him earlier. "I want to know if her resources are worth more than the hole she left in my team."

This was a dangerous assignment because it allowed both judgement calls and discrete skimming. Lots of ways to get in trouble if you got greedy or made an error. The look of betrayal on the sycophant's face flashed by so fast that most of the team missed it, but not the boss, and not Nico either. The boss slung Nico a micro-wink and then didn't pay any attention to him for the rest of the meeting.

Nico figured he was either doomed, or about to be promoted. With the boss it was kind of hard to tell.

As he walked back to his office, he found his mind wandering to his plans for that evening, when he would have time to review his research.

When Nico started looking for the lost forest, he had begun with side-by-side analysis of ancient architectural blue-prints, folk-site mapping and old salvager records. This was tedious but satisfying work. He gradually narrowed the potential megacity exits to the lost forest down to seventy-three possibilities. Now that the research part of the plan was complete, it was time for the actual physical exploration. But he was much more comfortable with dissecting old-data records than salvaging; this was the part he'd dreaded all along.

Nico pushed these thoughts out of his head and focused on work. Hours later, he leaned back in his chair to stretch his arms. It was late afternoon, not nearly close enough to quitting time.

There was an office party he had to make an appearance at. The boss's birthday wasn't something you could avoid, so that evening he attended and tried not to get pinned down in any conflicts or alpha games. He wore his mask and dutifully played his role. Nico ended up partying with the monsters once again and they never knew he wasn't one of them.

Some nights, he worried that the day would come when he wouldn't be able to distinguish between pretending to be a monster and being one—and that always upset him. But he attended such gatherings anyway. Office politics, you know. The whole thing made his stomach hurt.

Over the next few weeks, he settled into a routine that combined work with his secret hunt, and exploring the lower regions became a pleasure.

One morning, he woke to find a grin plastered across his face. He didn't have to be at the office until late afternoon. Rising leisurely, he made hot tea and zapped a chocolate croissant. He took the time to enjoy breakfast, then strapped up and walked to his back door. He had trained extensively, building strength for the Paradise hunt and this day he would need it. Butterflies began running amok in his belly, but he defiantly exited his apartment and made his way down to the eightieth floor. He was going to check out Door Eight.

Nico squeezed his lanky frame through a broken elevator door, and out into the abandoned corridor that no one had been down in centuries, if the luminescent mold and crumbled security gates meant anything. He pushed back his rebellious black hair from his face, grinning widely in growing excitement. Maybe this was it!

The lower levels of the mega-city had been abandoned long ago when a particularly deadly tox-mold bloom spread through them. Then the Rat armies discovered it was edible, and that was the end of the mycelium invasion. The Rat armies thrived for a while, which became a different kind of problem when they began looking for new sources of food. The humans weren't happy about their solution.

As he made his way down the shadowy corridor, he thought for a moment that he heard the patter of many small feet but dismissed the thought. The Rats were long dead and gone, weren't they? He found himself wondering just how smart they had been before their race was wiped out by management.

These days all the best apartments and offices were way upstairs anyway, although "ghosts", (ex-employees and illegal immigrants) were occasionally spotted in the lower levels. Every so often, upper-middle-management would organize ghost hunts down there for fun and games. Nico was glad that he wasn't senior enough to be invited to those parties. It was bad enough to see new trophies hanging on his boss's "I love me" wall when they had the Tuesday meetings.

Nico's implant map showed that the next section of the corridor had collapsed, completely obscuring anything further on. That was okay, he was prepared. He had recently obtained an upgrade, installed in his implant so he could process an additional Signal stream. Now he could run an eye-gnat remotely in real-time, seeing everything it did. Nico loved the small-tech.

The air felt humid and heavy here with the earthy scent of wild mushrooms and chalk. He watched the new-data stream intently as the tiny eye-gnat swooped out from behind his right ear and into a crevice in the debris. It began making its way to the target, an unusually fortified doorway that had survived the test of time. Twice, the miniature eye-gnat had to burn tiny, smoking holes in debris blocking the way. Eventually it was there, at the airlock. Nico realized he was holding his breath and forced himself to breath. Then he began carefully burning a pinhole through the sealed hatch.

His shoulders slumped as he saw burning-hot wastelands on the other side of the door. He resealed the mini-excavations on his way out.

Nico checked the time. He had to be at the office in less than an hour, so he trotted his way upstairs, stopping only long enough for a quick fresher visit and to pull on a clean shirt.

"Bonus to whoever can explain to me why our revenues are contracting instead of moving into new markets and taking new ground," the boss bellowed, sweeping his view from employee to employee. Everyone knew that to meet his eyes at times like these was taken as a challenge—and nothing good came of that.

"It only looks that way from a certain viewpoint! We are actually increasing $creds in an alternative..." the accounting guy stuttered to an uneven stop, his glorious work of fiction stillborn as he wilted under the boss's glare. This didn't distract the bad-boss a bit; he continued walking over to casually take the executive by the neck. After glaring into his about-to-be-demoted underling's eyes for a beat, he jerked him to his feet, and the victim had the nerve to begin cursing him viciously. The boss pushed the accounting guy into the waiting security team's arms, who vanished efficiently as usual, and straightened his tie.

For a second, Nico wished he could tell off the boss like that, but he could never be as brave as the accounting guy.

"Nigel is transferred to the Waste Management Division. Post a job opening in accounting," the boss directed the Human Resources manager. "Who else has an idea?" he asked, glaring at his team, waiting for someone else to speak up.

Finally, 'someone' did.

"There is no 'new ground' up here anymore. Every miserable block has been squabbled over for centuries. The only 'new ground' to be had is downstairs. I'm talking about going below the ninetieth story. No one is defending it aside from vermin and ghosts. We need to go in full-industrial and decontaminate every meter, then fortify and build new businesses and apartments. Everywhere else is old and tired. You want new, this is it," Nico found himself bluntly saying. Everyone stared at him, quite unused to hearing him speak up like that. He usually kept to the background; it was safer.

Somehow his mask had slipped, and he had inadvertently told the truth!

"Ha! Finally, a smart one with some backbone! Good, this is the kind of exchange of ideas that we excel at!" the boss declared, but no one was fooled. Within minutes it had become the boss's idea, though he still remembered to drop a nice bonus in Nico's implant. He also put Nico in charge of the project, which was even better. Now he would be able to search under the guise of securing the reclaimed territory.

The boss also set him up to be responsible if the plan failed, of course. Nico just hoped he'd find the right doorway before that happened, otherwise, he would end up transferred for sure.

Expanding into the lower levels turned out to be a great way to access areas formerly out of his reach. Nico spent every moment he could spare tracking down doors. Unfortunately, doorways Eleven through Fifty-One were a bust, and he was running out of excuses for disappearing. On the plus side, the new holdings were coming along nicely, and he was making quite a bit of $creds by directing construction jobs to the largest bribe, a traditional practice long established in the Corp-nations.

By this point the remaining possibilities were all upstairs, rather than down. Very low probability, but Nico refused to give up hope. The Doorway to Paradise had to be there out there somewhere! There weren't that many possibilities left, so he had to get lucky soon! Door sixty-three was sure to be it!

At first, exiting the mega-city from the two-hundred-fortieth story seemed highly improbable. What were you supposed to do—jump? Nico wondered as he forged his way through a long-forgotten warehouse district. He finally found it, down a dusty security corridor and in a cold antechamber.

Nico just stood there staring—the ancient, armored door was just laden with possibilities! Nico wore a fierce grin as he used his eye-gnat to get into the door's logics. After a moment, the large hatch slowly opened; the password overrides had been waiting in its auxiliary memory.

Nico peered over the portal's edge and saw a huge metallic slide that disappeared down into the dark. Then he saw the massive open-air elevator, obviously engineered to descend and climb the slope. He was willing to bet that it slid down all two-hundred plus stories before it came to a stop. This had to be it!

He clicked the time in his implant and winced when he realized he had to be at work in an hour. He immediately spun on his heels and retraced his steps, letting his eye-gnat detach to scan the antiquated tech for him and catch up later.

Nico was never late for work. It simply didn't pay to step into that den of hungry lions with an excuse to get schooled. Never, ever, look like prey around psychopaths.

Words Nico lived by.

The workday was filled with small problems and delays, but he couldn't stop thinking about his find. It was impossible to break free until late afternoon. Nico stopped by his apartment to change clothes on his way to the project site and was about to leave when his eye-gnat went into a fit and began dropping new-data feeds into his implant. He was under extensive surveillance! He quickly accessed his $cred records, saw they were jumping in numbers, and suddenly his stomach hurt.

He was being set up.

Ding! A chime in his implant delivered an order to attend a previously unannounced meeting with the boss in twenty minutes. He couldn't put together a defense in that time! He certainly wasn't ready to leave the mega-city yet—he thought he'd have weeks to psych himself up for the Door into Paradise! He wasn't even sure this was the one!

Nico told his stomach to stop churning, quieting the doubts and uncertainty that flooded his thoughts.

Yes, I'm scared, he admitted silently. I'm sure many of the managers at work have never experienced fear before, but I'm not a monster. Time to run if I want to live. He made himself move to his closet and open the door. He didn't have a choice really. He glanced once at his bed and then began strapping up.

The malachite doors blushed open like an innocent's first kiss; reluctant at first, then opening fully to the passion of life. Towering hemlock and Douglas pine in dark green and chocolate soaring to the sky. A velvet carpet of lime-green ferns under spreading pine branches loaded with forest green and pinecones. A huge alabaster moon hung over streams singing from the depths of the fern undergrowth, while a lonesome wind whipped evergreen boughs into a passionate sigh. It was everything Nico dreamed of, only brighter and real. It was perfect.

Nico was surprised to find that he wasn't scared anymore. After savoring that for a moment, he snorted and walked forward into his beloved dream.

Meanwhile back in the ancient megacity, Carmen was reading a bedtime story to Soli and her doll, from the beautiful old book that had mysteriously arrived earlier. It was called "Paradise Lost" and Soli's mother could already tell it was going to be her favorite.

"The Lost Forest" was first published in the Northwest Independent Writers Association 2019 Anthology.

Duck in a Dog Show

By Stephen Hagelin

Monroe

Evergreen State Fair

"Today's the day," Harriet thought as she sauntered through the gate, showing off her armband to the distracted youth who barred the way. Her mallard waddled dutifully behind her, giving a quack at the teenager, nearly causing him to choke on his vape. Feathers, her duck, wagged his head as they moved down the lane, and nearly tripped over an extension cord when he did a goose-necked double-take toward one of the carnival games. Harriet stifled a laugh at his expense when a particularly meaty little boy tossed a ring around a plastic duck's neck. She snapped her fingers and continued toward the back where the dog show would be held, confident that she'd be walking home with the prize.

Avoiding an oil-slicked puddle by the Gravitron ride, which whirled with its screaming occupants, a little too quickly, like a dented-quarter—she flicked her wrist and slowed it with a harmless charm just so. Now, passing it wouldn't mess up her hair. It had taken a long time to style it so that it looked worn and natural yet appealing. Harriet felt her hair with pride and pushed up one of its dark unwound curls as she passed a girl who was a bit too done-up. "Less is more," she explained, glancing down at Feathers, who was puffing along; she half imagined that he was sweating trying to keep up with her pace. She slowed; the organizers wouldn't mind if she missed the introductions of some of the regular pets.

There'd be setters, and Basset hounds, and Labs, and retrievers galore... but the look on their faces when she went in—well, it would almost be worth the price of her charm's ingredients. The garnet dust alone was worth, what, 12 dollars? Small price to pay for a bottle of Westland.

Only three days since she turned 21, and this was her chance to come of age in style!

Most girls would have their girlfriends take them out... but the only other girl her age was Mary, and there was no way in Hell she'd do something nice for her. No, the Monroe Magical Academy was too small. The only other student in their class was four!

As if he'd sensed her coming bad mood, Feathers quacked purposefully, and she looked up. Apparently, doing her hair had taken a lot longer than she'd thought, because the event organizer, a red-faced, fat man, who wore a poorly-attached and slightly off-colored toupee, was already standing in the center of the show floor giving a vegan dog treat to a rather disappointed chihuahua. The people in the stands applauded for whatever the little rat-dog had done, and it trotted off to its master intolerably pleased with itself.

A veritable child stopped her at the door, his messy hair straightened and combed over his face. "The stands are full miss," he said, giving Feathers a confused look. Feathers chuffed and looked away.

"I'm a participant. Harriet," she said self-importantly, scanning the crowd through the door.

"Oh, alright then. Can I see your entry-form?" he asked helpfully.

She stared at him. That worthless piece of paper was important? She'd thrown it in the trash! Eyes bulging, she replied, "I must have lost it," and she made a show of looking in her purse before she looked back at him with shoulders slumping. "I've got my duck right here!"

"I'm not supposed to just let people in," he explained, almost looking smug.

Swallowing her pride, she tried to flutter her eyes at him, using just the slightest bit of a charm to actually make it work.

He covered a laugh but relented anyway and waved her through. She went in, Feathers forgotten, beet red in the face for several reasons. Skirting the aisle, she spared a look at the arena, where a glossy black lab sat before the fat man, watching his mouth, not the biscuit in his stubby-fingered hand. Harriet stopped in her tracks and scanned the room. Three chairs away from her sat a beautiful young woman with flowing blond hair, in a form-fitting trench coat, wearing a smug grin.

"Eat, drink, and be Mary..." Harriet breathed angrily. Her duck was still at the door, so she snapped her fingers, and it padded over carelessly. She sat in her chair and pointedly avoided meeting Mary's taunting look.

"I think you should duck your tail between your legs and go home, Harriet," Mary commented coolly, watching her black lab as it leaped through one hoop, then another, and ran around a pattern of cones in an intricate dance; and the audience gave such appreciating responses, and the incessant notes of praise wafted into her ears like mosquitoes on a... she added a charm to keep mosquitoes away, and watched cheerfully as one landed on Mary's exposed neck.

The mosquito sizzled with an electric-blue pinprick of light, and the ash blew off in the breeze. Mary, it seemed, had warded herself just in case.

The lab climbed up a few stacked boxes and did something clever, so Harriet scoffed for good measure—but only earned a few odd looks from the other contestants. He cantered back down the boxes and sat obediently before the organizer, panting, but patient, until he was given the promised treat, and an unwarranted bout of applause as he ran back to his master and sat nobly on the chair beside her. It was just as well that she and Mary were separated by the animals, since they were content to ignore each other, though Bozo (as she referred to him) looked at Feathers in an awfully condescending way. It was all water off Feather's back, and he didn't care; he was a duck.

After Bozo's circus act, the people were disappointed when an untrained and wildly affectionate border collie pranced around the confused organizer, who tried to instruct it to sit down and to enlist the help of its owner to no avail. The collie's owner was a distracted 8-year-old who chased after it laughing. The crowd's disappointment dissipated and there was a chorus of "awws" and Harriet's heart sank as the organizer heaved his bulk up the blocks and around the cones, leading a jumping dog through the course, to open cheers and laughter.

The other dogs faired far better, and received far less praise, but none were as obedient as Bozo, or as loved as the collie; and she nearly fell out of her chair when she realized it was her turn next. The organizer stood in the center with a dog biscuit in hand, as he read "Feathers" from the list, and looked up in shock as the duck flew over and landed at his feet with a smug "quack".

"O-ooh! Well, um, let's see, I think, ah..." the organizer stammered, running a hand over his head, knocking off his toupee, "I don't think I've ever, really, seen..." He ran out of breath and labored to suck in another gulp of air before he decided to meet the reality of his situation with a cold, hard, gritty set to his teeth. He bent down and held the treat before the duck's beak and pointed to the set of cones. There'd be no leading this duck through them; Feathers snorted and waddled off, going around one, then another, and another, as he looped through the cones like a belt in a car engine.

This earned him some impressed mumbling in the crowd, and Harriet sat a little straighter in her seat just in case anyone looked in her direction. A duck in a Dog Show, well who'd ever heard of a thing like that!? She'd get this prize, tear off the foil, open it up, and take a quick swig right out of the bottle—just to rub it in Mary's snooty, stupid little face.

Feathers returned to the Awestruck Wonder, who'd recovered enough of his self-awareness to find his dirt and hay-covered toupee and slap it clumsily on his head. "Right!" He declared, rising triumphantly, as if he'd told the duck to do all that. It had taken weeks of preparation to get her duck in a row!

Her heart raced as he held a hoop just off the ground, and Feathers hopped through, and then, the organizer pointed to a series of hoops. They were arranged on different boxes at assorted height levels to really give some dynamics to the show. Feathers would not be bothered waddling up and down and hopping through all that. He simply ran toward the first hoop, flapped furiously, and flew in a tight circle, navigating all the hoops, before settling down to an open-mouthed audience. Silence reigned; a silky gray feather drifted to the ground.

Dumbfounded, the organizer held out the dog treat, as if he expected the duck to eat it, and Harriet laughed when Feathers' head snaked forward, and it bit the man on his thumb! A good number of the audience clapped when he jumped back and rubbed his sore hand with embarrassment, and they clapped until Feathers had flown back over and settled comfortably on the chair beside her, nestling his head in his fluffed feathers.

The wait, oh, the unbearable wait! They watched three more stupid animals stumble around the cones, and the last one, well, he just stole the treat and was dropped from the contest. At last, the organizer, more of a performer than any of the animals (indeed, he'd done the circuit himself more than once) brought out the three prizes: a bottle of Westland Whiskey, for the first-place winner, a basket with crackers and a wheel of Brie for the second place, and for third a large tin of kettle corn.

The Collie was ushered out with the little boy, and above the baying of the hysterical animal, the organizer's words were unintelligible; but to both Mary's and her relief, the boy was given the Brie and crackers.

"...not nearly old enough for his deserved prize..." he was saying to the applause and joy of everyone else. He pinned a large frilly blue ribbon on the boy's chest, and his idyllic story-book parents stood beside him glowing with pride.

Well, even if Feathers didn't take first, the Westland was still available.

"And now, for the Westland, for the most remarkable performance I have seen in a long time, and for his good manners and obedience, Mary Johnson, and her black lab Berlin!"

Mary didn't say anything. She didn't have to. She merely sauntered down the stairs, out onto the floor with her Black Stallion of a dog, to overwhelming approval.

Anything would have been better than seeing Mary delicately removing the foil at the cork, and unstopping it with her sultry smile, as she placed her nose over it. She was too proper to taste it there, but she met Harriet's eyes as she laughed and praised her dog with a few repeated 'who's my good boy's.

Nothing could be worse than hearing her name next. Feather's head peaked out of his wing, and he waddled abjectly beside her as if he were waddling to his grave. She stood beside Mary, blushing not with pride, but rage, as the Kirkland Signature tin of kettle corn was unceremoniously deposited in her hands.

"Such a spectacular show, truly!" The organizer declared, "I have to say that is the first time I have seen a duck participate, but it was well trained. Well done, Miss Harriet, well done." He looped the overlarge ribbon around Feather's neck, and leaned back with a smug, self-satisfied smile.

As the people cheered, and they all walked toward the exit, her familiar, Feathers, shrugged off the ribbon, leaving it where it fell, and commented in a perfectly pitched monotone: "this is degrading." No one else could hear him of course, but his, no her, humiliation was too much to bear.

Mary strutted out the door before them, sparing a haughty glance over her shoulder as she scratched Bozo's ear. Harriet, stomach churning at this new outrage, stared daggers at Mary and her stupid black dog, and her stupid bottle of whiskey, and her stupid coat and stupid good grades, and everything stupid she represented.

"This *is* degrading!" she whispered to her duck.

He gave a disheartened quack and fluttered up to perch on her shoulder. He at least could stomach the kettle corn, and she gave him a sideways, suspicious glance… he might not be sufficiently upset after all.

He stuffed his head in among her assuredly warm curls, and whispered so no one else could hear him, "At least she got second to that border Collie."

"Hmph," she replied, and decided not to say or think anything more of it, until she was safely back in the confines of her home.

"Duck in a Dog Show" was first published in the Northwest Independent Writer's Association 2018 Anthology.

Dream Sequence

by Suzanne Hagelin

At first there was a smell, a sickly-sweet odor in an aromatic fog, filling Weylah with unease bordering on alarm. It was followed by sharp pain in the back of her skull, as if a huge needle had punctured it. Then the pain vanished, and she could see a cloud, bluish with feathered streaks of red, and murky lights glimmering through. After a moment, the mist and the scent dispersed, but the taste of danger remained, leaving her mouth dry.

"Hold the flask on the back of your hand," Weylah heard. They were the first words she was aware of, almost like a dream. She glanced down at her hand where it lay on an armrest and saw a glass of sorts, half full of water, balancing on the back of her hand.

"Like this?" she asked as she took in more of her surroundings. A chair. That made sense. Armrests were usually attached to chairs. And they often looked just like this one when they were in an office or a clinic of some sort.

"That will be fine," someone said. She became aware of the clinic. All the normal aspects were there; a waiting area with children playing with some toys in the corner, and a reception desk with a non-descript person answering questions.

Was this right? Would she have someone instructing her in the lobby instead of an examination room? The scene twisted and began to morph.

Wait. This wasn't the lobby. That was a wall over there, not the play area.

She looked back down at her hand. The glass was pink, and the water bubbly. *Am I thirsty?* she wondered. Sometimes she dreamed of water when… was this a dream?

Weylah jerked her head around looking for the source of the words she'd been listening to. She was alone in the room. The motion made the flask wobble and splash water onto her fingers. Her brief concern was swept away by the conviction that it didn't matter. Yanking her hand out, she grabbed the glass without spilling a drop. *Ha!* she thought, bringing it to her lips. Cold, fresh water.

She couldn't taste it.

She set the glass down and rose to her feet. Was that a commotion outside? Or maybe in the lobby? A low rumbling sound and faint voices carried toward her from the distance, little whines in the wind.

With one step she reached the door and pulled it open.

The scene that met her eyes was chaotic, beyond her ability to grasp. She stared around in a stupor, taking it all in, struggling to make sense of it. It was as if gravity didn't make sense anymore, and up and down wouldn't stay in place. Things were whirling around and slamming into buildings or cars or whatever those moving objects were. Not a tornado. That would have some sense of motion she could interpret, fitting into a spinning, whipping pattern. This was all mixed up.

She took a step out into the wild and found her foot landing on solid ground that stayed where it should. "What is going on?" she yelled into the wind, the words were swallowed by the noise.

She took a few more steps and realized she could walk, and the visual distortion wasn't a true interpretation of what surrounded her. There were wind and noise, but as she walked, she could make out a bit of sidewalk under her feet, and here and there, people, sitting or standing motionless staring up at the mess.

"What is all this?" she asked a kid who crouched with his arms in a semicircle.

"Quiet!" he hissed at her. "I'm trying to get it to trust me. Back away and go around behind me!" There was nothing she could see nearby but she imagined an animal, maybe injured. He was trying to coax it into his embrace so he could take care of it. For a moment she was tempted to squat next to him and help. After all, she was pretty good with animals.

No, she shook her head. The roar of the storm blasted her again. There was nothing there and she didn't intend to take that tangent. This was clearly a dream and she wanted to know what it all meant.

The turbulence crystalized into a city street with a mighty storm beating at the buildings and buffeting the people, like herself, who were foolish enough to be out in it. The whole purpose of the windblasts seemed to be to force her inside. Anywhere.

She stubbornly stayed outdoors, shivering in the cold, getting drenched by the rain. Had it been raining at first? She didn't know.

Then the flashes began, like lightning but all wrong. It didn't arc from land to sky or from sky to land. They sliced sideways, at angles, sometimes in single thread-like beams, sometimes in scattered explosions. Like fireworks.

Weylah stopped walking and stared. The people she had been passing were being vaporized, one by one. The wave of death rolled up the street, taking down buildings as it neared her, but no one noticed except for her. Everywhere she looked, people were busy, preoccupied with little things that didn't matter, and the ripple of destruction took them without warning.

She was looking right at it, her mouth wide open, shrieking into the wind, but she was unable to hear anything besides the roar it made, and never saw the flash when it pierced her.

It all faded.

Weylah opened her eyes and found herself in the room again, sitting in the chair. Only this time, there was no flask on her hand. An attendant sat across from her, eyes on a pad where he tapped and clicked, making notes.

A clock was ticking nearby. *That means time is moving forward*, she thought.

She looked at the attendant, waiting for him to lift his eyes so she could speak. He never did. She spoke anyway.

"Excuse me," she said, using her polite manner. "Can I ask what I'm waiting for?"

The man glanced up at her, a distinctly smug look on his face, but said nothing. He went back to his notes.

"Am I waiting on results? I'm not sure what…"

"The test is over," he said, gesturing toward a passageway on her right that led to a sunny glass door.

She looked down the hall with the strong impression that it led to waking up. Then turned to her left to look at the door she had gone out earlier in the dream.

The attendant ignored her.

Normally, she would prefer to wake up, especially in this kind of dream, but something made her hesitate. Nightmares bring terror—but she wasn't afraid, just more alert, aware of both realms while sleeping. And there was an underlying tension that triggered something deeper than dream fear.

She jumped to her feet and ran toward the door to her left.

"Not that way," a voice behind her called.

She ignored it and pulled open the door to the outside.

The streets she had seen before awaited her and a storm was kicking up. It began moaning and slamming loose doors, knocking things over, whipping trash and debris around. It was almost as if the dream had started over and she was stepping into it earlier than she had the first time.

She made her way down the sidewalk, passing people occupied with various mindless pursuits like watching a butterfly, playing with a yo-yo, kicking a can, scratching patterns in the dirt, trying to catch a skittish cat.

"Hey!" she found herself saying as she turned to look at the kid she had noticed the first time. "What happened to it?" Inside she was wondering, *did her mind fill in the cat or was it easier to see because the storm hadn't blown out of control yet?*

"I don't know," he said. "She ran out the door and she's never done that before. She's really scared..." He circled his arms and squatted, cornering the cat. It wavered between looking at him fondly and staring over his shoulder. Then its hair rose on end and its tail puffed as the noise of the tempest began to increase. The sidewalk underneath them swayed and dipped, like the entire city was inside a rocking cradle.

"Come on," Weylah patted the boy's arm. "Let her go. We've got to run before the full brunt of the storm hits."

He looked up at her in confusion. "The what?" he said, and his eyes bulged, as if he hadn't noticed the noise till that moment. "What's happening?" The cat ran past him into the distance.

"Come on!" she yelled, and they both ran the same direction.

The wave of destruction, crashing and exploding behind them, poured down the streets in their wake. Most of the people they passed seemed to be unaware of it. Weylah slapped at their arms or pushed them as she ran past, calling them, but unable to slow down to try to wake them up.

There was no time.

"Come on! Come on!" the kid screamed, kicking into high gear and tearing down the road faster than her. The skies overhead were getting darker, billowing with solid clouds of storm. Or was it like ash from a volcano?

The roar grew louder till it shook her body as it vibrated through her. She should have been terrified, but wasn't. There was still that strong sense of *something else*.

She never saw the end. She just stopped vibrating and opened her eyes again in the clinic chair. The attendant was sitting in the same place, still tapping the pad. She stared at him for a moment, knowing he was aware of her, waiting for him to say something, or just look up. He didn't. But she knew he wasn't feeling quite as smug as he had the first time.

This is my dream, she considered, *in my head*.

He paused, finger poised over the pad, listening. Aware. *Somewhere in my brain, I know what he's typing.*

The attendant's eyes lifted to hers and glanced away. He definitely wasn't looking as smug as he had before.

She jumped to her feet and ran for the door to the left again. This was a puzzle, and she was going to figure it out.

"Wait!" a voice called, "Well done! You've passed the test!"

Outside, the buildings, sidewalks, roads, and people were all the same as before, but not everyone was doing the same thing as before. Some of them had shifted. They must be on a different loop, if that was the right word, and her story was the only one repeating. The woman with the butterfly had coaxed it onto her finger. The man with the yo-yo had stopped swinging it around and was studying the pattern etched in its side. The old guy kicking the can had disappeared.

The kid who had tried to catch the cat was watching her as she approached. As if he had been waiting for her.

"You!" he said.

"Where's your cat?" she countered, glancing over her shoulder to see if the wave had started.

"She got away last time," he said, backing up as if he wanted her to run with him again.

"Did the wave get you?" she asked as she started jogging next to him. They passed several of the same people as before.

"Yeah. I don't know."

A woman scrolling on her phone raised her eyebrows in recognition as they went by. "Aren't you the one who pushed me last time?" she asked Weylah, "Why did you do that?"

The dream was looping but the people weren't.

That was important.

"We've got to get away from the storm," the kid answered before she could.

They began collecting people as they ran. There were at least twelve as the storm began raging and overtaking them. At the last second before it vaporized them, she turned around to look into it, wanting to see what it was, what lay behind the power.

Time slowed. Her body twisted in slow motion and her eyes focused on the broiling storm cloud, the shock wave. She planted her feet and burrowed into it with her mind as well as her gaze. And she saw something behind the destruction.

A being. Multiple beings, running along with lasers in their hands, gunning down everything in their path. They had rectangular torsos with faces in the middle and they seemed like they were having fun.

"NO!" she yelled at them, unable to hear the sound from her own lips.

One of them almost ran into her and paused as if startled.

She closed her eyes. The crash. The flash. The quiet. The room.

There was the attendant again and he wasn't tapping notes this time. She was back in the chair. She focused on the pad in his hands and projected her understanding toward it. *All is going well*, it said at the top. *Apathy is an easily spread substance. Thoroughly effective at rendering them helpless.*

Something in her knew that the words hadn't been in English—and she had supplied the translation.

A minor difficulty... followed, after a break in the notes, *subject behaving erratically. No need for concern...*

Weylah was pretty sure she was the 'subject' and 'apathy' was the cloud over the minds of the people in her dream.

"Who are you?" she asked with less force than she had meant to project, feeling a little weary from the running around. *I should sit here for a moment to recover*, she thought.

The attendant's eyes didn't lift up to look at her, but he was *intensely* aware of her. Why would she dream of him? What did he mean in her mind?

She rose to her feet calmly this time, took a step and snatched the pad out of his hands. It was blank. "It is not blank," she said. Words began to form on the surface in not quite legible shapes and flourishes that resembled letters but meant nothing.

"I can read it," she said, and she recognized the meaning she had already discerned even though the lines on the screen remained unintelligible. Handing the pad back to him, she turned and walked toward the door on the left again. He didn't try to stop her.

Outside, the kid was waiting for her. He must have figured out which door was hers which struck her as being very cool. "What are we going to do?" he asked. "We can't just keep running."

She looked at him carefully, studying his face, wanting to remember it when she awoke—because he *was* a real person, not just the product of a dreaming mind. She was sure of it.

"What's your name?" she asked.

"Digo. You?"

"Weylah… or Wey…" She wasn't sure why she added the nickname of her childhood.

"Oh," he said.

"Did you look at them?" She faced the direction the storm always came from.

"I was going to… when you turned around," he answered, his eyes widening as he stood beside her, facing the same way. "But all I saw was the lightning strike and you puffed into a swirl of smoke…" He gestured with his hands, pantomiming the explosion. "Then I was gone again."

"Where do you wake up after that?"

"My room… I'm supposed to be straightening it but the cat…" he scratched his head and scrunched his nose as if he had to add pressure to his skull in order to figure it out.

"Look out!" Weylah cried out. The tossing clouds and torrents of wind were upon them. "There! There!" she added in a screech that barely carried over the noise.

"I see!" he yelled back in his boyish voice.

The beings were running toward them, waving triangular loops of glowing metal, shooting out bolts of blue and white from the points, sometimes one, sometimes all three as it rotated in their grasp. Their faces gaped with triangular mouths and no teeth.

One ran up to the boy and another ran up to Weylah. Again, time slowed down. She was sure it was the same being as before, grinning, stretching its triangle till it filled the rectangular body with a black maw. The first time, it had been startled by her but now it chose her. Long fibrous strands hung from the top of its rectangular body like fringe. They were cords that turned their tips to look at her.

63

Eyes, she thought, hundreds of light receptacles scanning her.

Digo was backing away, one step at a time, just out of reach of the being's arm. It wasn't shooting at him. The one in front of her wasn't shooting either. It had stopped at the edge of her personal space and was twirling the laser gun on a spindly limb of some kind.

There was something repulsive about it and it made her angry. She shouted words at it, not sure what they were, challenging it. And as she continued voicing her defiance, she shoved her fist out in front of her, almost brushing its waving cords. The being shrunk back, the cords trembled—and she stepped toward it.

One punch, with no power in it. The kind that feels like you hardly moved because part of your brain knows you're sleeping, and the arm isn't moving. But the rage she felt was real. Her fist pushed up to it and sank into its gaping mouth, brushing against a cloudy fuzz that expanded like a bubble. The being exploded into chalky dust with streaks of several bright colors, pink, green, blue, like carnival ribbons. Like finger-paint colors.

In that one spot, the storm ceased, and time sped up again.

She whirled around, looking for Digo. He was staring at her in astonishment, the word "What?" half formed in his mouth when the being pursuing him blasted him.

Then Weylah was vaporized as well, struck from behind by another being.

She opened her eyes.

The attendant was sitting very still, holding onto the pad tightly with both hands, staring at it.

Invasion Tactics, the header read.

He couldn't just hang out in her dream without giving her access to those notes. He should've thought of that. The attendant closed his eyes. "You may depart," he said, and for the first time she noticed that his lips didn't move when he spoke.

Desensitization is very effective... proceeding according to plan...

"What are you doing to us?" she glowered at him.

Then the gist of the whole document suddenly pierced her understanding, and she knew that this was not just a dream of an experiment with imaginary creatures.

She jumped to her feet.

How would a race of aliens test the possibility of invasion? What if they were approaching humans in dreams to see how they would handle an attack?

"Wait right there!" she commanded the attendant and ran to the door on the left as fast as she could, *knowing* he was stranded in her mind until she let him go.

Digo was holding a bat. "There's no way they're getting me this time," he yelled. "Here!" He tossed her a stick about three feet long.

"Quick!" Weylah called out as she caught it. "Let's round up as many people as we can before they get here." With that they started down the street, slapping, knocking, shoving people to get their attention. Some of them were already awake and aware of them.

"No, don't run!" they were crying. "Fight! We can do it!"

The aliens had created a scenario where people met their end in a puff of vapor, because it fit their own experience of extinction. *This* was what death looked like for them.

The rumbling started and the wind kicked up.

"Come on!" Weylah and Digo yelled to each other as they sprinted into the wind swinging their weapons.

Clouds of color burst in their wake as they barreled into the crowd of creatures. The storm dispelled in bubbles of quiet as the dust of each one settled to the ground. All around them people were fighting, and the noise of the battle spread down streets and blocks and across the neighborhood till the clouds were gone and a mighty cheer burst from the throats of the victors.

Sunshine began to brighten around them.

"No!" Weylah cried out with all her might. "Not yet!! Don't wake up! We're not done!" But all around her, people were vanishing and waking up from the dream.

"Digo!" she called, searching all around. But he was gone, too.

The light was encroaching on her mind, but she turned her back to it. *Not yet.* She wasn't about to leave that attendant lurking in her dream state. Where was the door she had come out of? She wandered down the chalk-covered road in the direction that felt right and soon found it.

She stepped back into the waiting room where the attendant waited, riveted to the spot where she had left him.

Weylah sat down across from him resting the stick on her knees. He stared down at his pad but was observing her keenly.

How many of them had come testing people in their dreams before this night? Was this the first time or was she just one peon in a batch, in a stream of batches, of dreaming people?

Humans around the world were falling asleep as the planet turned and their homes entered the dark side of the world. Like a wave. They were accustomed to letting their minds ramble or stress or venture into unknown realms. Would they find a storm threatening?

She stared at the attendant. "How many?"

Many, she sensed his thought. He couldn't hide it from her. He had exposed himself when he entered her dream.

"How long?"

The answer was simultaneously past and future. She saw the Earth cycling in orbit halfway around the sun, turning on its axis. Half a year. *A few more planet rotations… a few more days to go.*

66

"Till what?" she insisted though her voice sounded calm—and she *knew* what.

Till we move in. He turned his eyes toward her as if he were unable to stop himself, as if he had more than two eyes. His hair seemed pulled toward her, and he was vibrating.

Somewhere, a mass of rectangular brutes was stretching and warming up. Laughing, practicing their target shooting, getting ready for the day that would soon come. This wasn't the first species they had conditioned not to resist. It had been a successful tactic a number of times.

"Why?"

The attendant's face was looking smug again. Its eyes were glowing a little and its head grew more horizontally oblong than before, though still humanoid. The illusion it had kept for her was fading. She saw another image in its mind, not rectangular like the parody of an alien they had decided to portray in the storm, but an aged, desiccated, barely moving lump of a body. Their real bodies, wherever they were out there, had been lovely once long ago. Now, they were nothing but chalk held together by thought, hardly moving, breathing husks at the end of their usefulness… soon to be vacated.

"Will you swipe your stick at me?" it asked as its mouth triangulated and shaped words laced with humor.

She could. He would turn into a puff of chalky dust and her dream would end. She would wake up and enter the real world where all this would seem distant and foolish. They would move on to the next batch and start again.

"I could," she replied, leaning forward. He shrunk back a bit, but the arrogance never left him.

Sometimes invasions were drawn out, bloody affairs.

Sometimes they were quick and unexpected.

Weylah didn't believe this was just a dream. From the beginning, the being had tried to get her to go out the door on the right and wake up. And each time she ran out the left door, they began the experiment again. If this was a precursor to an invasion, what were they afraid of? Why didn't they just overpower or imprison her?

"If you do not leave the dream, you will die here," it said, its corded fringe waving in the air, looking at her.

Sometimes invasions were high risk.

And sometimes... they backfired.

Weylah rose slowly to her feet, gripping the stick tightly in her hands. The being's face flicked back to a human shape again with alarm etched in its features. It sensed her intent and began screeching.

"Where is the door *you* came through?" She set her lips in a grim line. The link the attendant had made to access her mind—the one he didn't want her to notice—was open into *his* mind.

"Abort! Abort!" it began screaming, wheeling its limbs in a chaotic frenzy.

Then she saw the third door, straight behind him. Three strides took her there and she pulled it open with enough force to rip it off the hinges. The tempest raged out there in violent tosses of night-colored storm clouds and a wispy funnel shaped light snapped around in the center.

"You'll never survive!!" the alien was wailing as a sucking wind pulled it out the opening.

"Neither will you," she said as she gritted her teeth and stepped through after it.

Dream Sequence was first published in the Northwest Independent Writers Association 2019 Anthology.

Genetic Shift

by Denise Kawaii

Rain slapped the leaded glass window above Anna's desk. The heavy New Jersey rain nearly drowned out the squeal of the mail slot's hinges when the postman shoved letters through.

Anna set aside the research paper she was transcribing with a sigh. Working in a laboratory would be more exciting if she were allowed to ignore the office work and get her hands dirty with research instead. She smoothed a fold in her skirt, unfurling a hitch in the fabric before stooping to pick up the soggy letters scattered just inside the door. Anna strode past her desk, down the hallway, and into the lab, searching for a towel to mop up the mail's trailing ink before it washed away from the envelopes completely. Finding the least greasy cloth in the room, she returned to her desk and laid the letters across the battered wood.

There were several smart looking envelopes with colorful embellishments for Doctor Einstein, of course. His fame hadn't been dampened by the war on the horizon in the slightest. Indeed, his opinions seemed to be all that mattered to people in high places. Two letters, less illustrious, were written out to Mister Curtis, the lab technician. Only one, a utility bill, had Mister Charles Edison's name stamped above the address.

When she discovered the last envelope, she was surprised to see her own name typed in neat, block text. Despite the pulpy mire the rest of the mail threatened to disintegrate into, the piece addressed to her was hardly damp. It only bore a pair of small stains soaked into either side of the address where it had pressed against another piece of mail.

Anna would let the men's letters dry before she delivered them to the receptacles in their assigned workspaces. She plucked her own letter from the desk, turning it over in her hands and wondering who might have sent it. There was no return address, and the envelope was missing the customary three cent postage.

Either the post office made an error in not charging the sender, or the letter hadn't been sent through the mail service at all.

Anna's heart fluttered as she ripped the envelope open. The thick, cream paper smelled faintly of metal and glue. The scent took her back to the Radium Institute in Paris. She'd only stayed a few weeks the summer of her fifteenth birthday, assisting her mother briefly in the labs. Her mother, Irène, had insisted on assessing Anna's comprehension of the sciences firsthand. Anna didn't know why, but once her mother was pleased with her service, she'd promptly sent her to study abroad.

Despite the familiar scent, this letter wasn't from the Radium Institute. There was no romantic flourish of French language written within the paper's folds. Instead, it was typed with the same dull accuracy as the address on the envelope. Pushing aside the nostalgic hope of word from her estranged family aside, Anna read.

April 22nd, 1943

Dear Miss Joliot-Curie,

I trust this letter finds you well. In recent days, your family name has become central to my work.

It seems our futures were bound together before we were born. Now, destiny calls. I have answered, and I pray you will do the same.

In the course of your work, you may have heard whispers of recent government interest in the nuclear sciences. Or, perhaps, lectures about them due to the outspoken nature of your employers. If, however, Albert and Charles have kept their opinions from you, I regret I am unable to enlighten you via this letter.

What I offer instead is an opportunity of utmost importance, secrecy, and national security. In short, a position suited to your talents and lineage. Less letter-sorting and more time playing with instrumentation.

I am aware that you received high marks from your tutor, and that your work with Albert has been both professional and discreet. It is these traits, coupled with the Curie name, which allow me to offer you this position.

Should you accept this proposal, please go directly to Henry's Leather Works at 15th and Main. Ask to speak with Mister Kitchen. He will instruct you further.

Whether you choose to accept, or not, it is your duty to destroy the contents of this letter via fire, flood, or chemical disintegration.

Kindest regards,

J. Oppenheimer

Anna's hand gripped her throat as she read the letter again. She had never received mail at the lab before, and it was signed by one of the men Doctor Einstein had been ranting about just this morning. What could such a man want from her?

A loud crash filled the air. Anna jumped from her seat, bumped into the corner of her desk, and caused the damp letters to leap across the desktop. Mister Curtis ran toward her, the tails of his lab coat blooming with orange flame.

"Out of my way, girl! Out of my way!" he shouted. His flailing arm landed against her shoulder, pushing her back into her chair with a short cry of surprise. He rushed through the office toward the front door, screaming bloody murder. He grabbed the handle and swung the door open wildly on its hinges as he raced out into the deluge.

Anna rose from her seat and hurried to the door, which flapped in the howling wind. Outside, steaming with heat and fury, Mister Curtis tore his flame-ridden coat from his shoulders and flung it to the ground. He stomped the now-smoldering cloth into a puddle with a flourish few other men could manage. The torrential rain cascaded down the soot-streaked back of his pale blue button-down shirt like a river. It was but a moment before the remnants of the fire were smothered betwixt the weight of his heel and the wet pavement.

Anna snatched an umbrella from the stand just inside the door. She opened it and hurried outside to hold it over Mister Curtis's head. "What happened?"

"It's that blasted burner!" Mister Curtis shouted. Several people walking by turned to peer under their caps and umbrellas at the commotion. "It's gone haywire *again*! I tried to shut it off when it overheated, but when I grabbed the valve it knocked the blasted thing from the table, right onto my coat!"

"Is it still lit?" Anna asked. She felt her eyes widen and her heart skipped a beat. She looked through the doorway into the building but didn't see flames licking the framework of the hallway that led into the lab.

72

"How the hell should I know?" he sputtered.

Anna thrust the umbrella into Mister Curtis's hand and abandoned him for the building. She ran inside, down the barren hall, and into the lab proper.

Mister Curtis's worktable was charred, and the Bunsen burner swung freely; a pendulum and bonfire combined into to one. Its flame fell and billowed as the gas line choked and relieved itself with each swing against the desk's edge. The line leading to the gas tank was mere inches away from the swinging flame.

Burning coat or not, Anna cursed the lab tech for running off without closing the valve.

"What a mess," Anna grumbled to herself, twisting the regulator's handle closed. The flame died on the wild burner, and she pulled on a thick heat-resistant glove before grasping it to turn it upright. Mister Curtis, wet shirt clinging to his chest like a second skin, came into the lab and dropped the remains of his coat into the waste receptacle.

"That's all the work we'll do today, I'm afraid. I must shut up shop until I can report this accident to Albert and Charles." Mister Curtis shook his head, a look of misery written on his face.

"Are you sure? I can help you put things right. Well, aside from the lab coat, of course."

"Thank you for the offer, but it's better if you're not involved," Mister Curtis said. His twitching lips betrayed his lack of confidence. "This is my third incident this month, you know. There is no sense in subjecting you to the lecture Albert and Charles will unleash the moment they hear about it. Please, tidy up whatever mess I created in the office, then lock the door behind you when you leave."

Anna nodded. Normally she'd insist she finish her shift. Her portion of the rent wouldn't pay itself, after all. But the mysterious letter from Mister Oppenheimer tugged at her. She returned to her desk, locked her unfinished transcriptions in the bottom drawer, and pressed her forefinger against one of the letters still lying on her desk. The thick envelope squelched as moisture leaked from its sides.

Anna returned to the lab, finding Mister Curtis disassembling the faulty Bunsen burner. He'd rolled up the sleeves of his button-down shirt. Streaked with marks from the fire, still soaked through with rain, he looked more like an auto mechanic than a lab rat.

"Sir," Anna said, "the mail got soaked through in the rain, and it hasn't dried out yet. Do you want me to deliver it to you and the others as it is?"

Mister Curtis shook his head and waved her off. "Leave it to dry. Whatever news the letters hold can wait until tomorrow."

Anna nodded and returned to the front office. She picked the wet mail up from her desktop, chuckling at the perfect rectangular shadows of moisture left on the wood where each letter had rested. Carefully, she propped each piece on the windowsill above her desk, leaving room for air to flow around the paper to aid in their drying overnight.

Finally, she plucked her own letter from the floor, where it had fallen during the excitement of Mister Curtis's flaming coat. She froze for a moment, remembering the letter's instruction to destroy it by fire or flood. She had read those words mere seconds before Mister Curtis's jacket had gone ablaze and was submerged in a stream of rainwater outside.

For a moment, it seemed like more than just coincidence.

Anna brushed the prickly feeling of unease from the back of her neck. Now was not the time to let her imagination run away with her. She tucked the letter in her dress hip pocket and bent to retrieve her handbag from below her desk. The letter slipped out and fell to the floor. She picked it back up, realizing it might be dangerous to let it wiggle its way out again.

Anna looked over her shoulder toward the lab, making sure Mister Curtis was still occupied. There was no movement near the door, so she returned to her chair and pulled the hem of her dress to her knees, turning the fabric over and tracing her fingers along the seams.

Irène Joliot-Curie hadn't been active in her daughter's upbringing by anyone's standards. In fact, for most of Anna's life, her mother had been content to pretend she didn't exist. It wasn't until she received reports that her daughter had outpaced her science tutors that Irène had shown any interest in motherhood. And then, in an uncharacteristic act of care, Irène had taken Anna under wing and ensured she had everything she needed to be a successful woman of the world. When Anna began working, Irène had shipped several specially tailored dresses to Anna, including the one she wore now. Each dress had come with a variety of concealed pockets hidden among their skirts, sleeves, and bodices. Initially, Anna had found the dresses' construction odd. But she quickly came to understand the convenience of the curious feature.

With her dress skirt turned inside-out over her thighs, she found one of two hidden pockets. She slipped the letter inside and secured it with a small hook and loop that could be tucked invisibly along the stitching. Anna had just dropped her skirt back to her ankles when the lab tech entered.

"Oh! I thought you'd already gone," said Mister Curtis.

"I was just on my way out," Anna answered quickly. She ducked her head beneath her desk once more, retrieving her handbag. She rose from her chair and moved casually to the door where she slipped into her overcoat and retrieved the umbrella Mister Curtis had returned to the stand.

"I hope you don't get into too much trouble over the Bunsen burner. Maybe you'll get lucky, and they'll buy you a new one." Anna dug around in her handbag for her key.

"They'll bluster and howl for a while, but I'm sure they'll forgive me one more transgression." Mister Curtis moved to the door. "Don't worry about locking up. I'll take care of it."

Anna nodded a brief farewell. She opened the door, unfolded her umbrella, and walked out into the world while Mister Curtis shut and secured the door behind her.

Even with the downpour battering her umbrella and chill wind whipping up her skirt, Anna felt a strong urge to go anywhere but home. She couldn't feel the physical weight of the envelope hidden under her dress, but its message weighed heavily on her mind. She tilted her head, trying to remember the address inside the letter. She could go there, find out what this job offer was all about. But should she go alone?

She unfolded the page in her mind, but she couldn't focus on what it said. If only she'd taken the time to memorize the instructions! With a frown, she decided her forgetfulness would buy her time in deciding what to do. It would be best to be cautious, even though she was dying to know more about Mister Oppenheimer and his secretive job offer. She picked up her skirt in one hand to keep it out of the splattering rain and turned her feet toward home.

By the time she made it to the end of the block, the storm washed away her sense of adventure and she thanked the stars her flat was nearby. She'd be soaked through if she lived any farther away. Her pace quickened and while she thanked Doctor Einstein for every opportunity he'd given her, she secretly grumbled that the small salary she received wasn't enough for frequent trolley rides, and hiring a car was out of the question.

A few minutes later, Anna rushed up the stairs to her flat, fumbling her keys with shivering hands while she worked the lock to let herself in. The second the door opened, she was through it and quickly bolted it shut again, sagging against the worn wood while she caught her breath.

She worked herself free from her soggy jacket and tossed it and the umbrella atop a messy pile of discarded clothing shoved into a nearby corner. Free from the weight of the jacket, Anna flung herself onto the threadbare sofa. She hiked up the wet folds of her skirt, not bothering to be the least bit ladylike now that she was alone. She searched the fabric to find the secret pocket. There was a buzz of excitement in her ears, and her hands trembled with anticipation when she retrieved the letter. The pocket had kept the paper dry, even though the outer layer of the skirt was soaked with water and grime.

Carefully, she opened the envelope and unfolded the letter on the sofa's arm beside her. She traced the lines of text while she read and wondered why the man called Oppenheimer sent send it to her. Was her name, her parent's lineage, worth that much to him?

It could be dangerous for a single woman to move about the city without a friend and would be scandalous if people in certain social circles found out she met a man in secret. But how could she explain her excitement, this budding desire to embrace the unknown to her flatmate, Margaret? And if not Margaret, then who would she tell? She didn't know anyone else in town, aside from the men at the lab. Anna wasn't well practiced in social expectations, but even she knew that asking her employer to assist her in inquiring about another job was bad form.

The cushions embraced her as she slouched lower on the sofa. If only she had some family to lean on. She had thought when her half-sister Hélène was born that they'd grow to be one another's champions. But when the sweet girl arrived in society, and was well-received by the entire world, Anna was once again brushed aside. She read in the newspapers about her mother's travels with Hélène, and then her baby half-brother Pierre, and wished she could have a life grand enough to capture her mother's attention.

But that was then. Now, Anna was a woman, ready and willing to strike out on her own. Yes, her mother had sent her here to work with Doctor Einstein and his partners, but there was nothing keeping her from making a name for herself. Maybe one day her mother would read about her in the papers, and wish she'd been a part of Anna's grand adventures.

It was then, in the wistful remembering of a childhood left behind that Anna decided she was going to the address listed in the letter and would seek out the adventure hinted at there. But she wouldn't be stupid about it.

She extracted herself from the sofa and moved through the sitting room, opening the lid to what had once been a writing desk. From the jumble of experimental equipment, handcrafted tools, and spare parts inside, she retrieved a device of her own invention. It was a simple contraption; a small, pressurized chamber, filled with a hearty amount of ground chili pepper suspended in an emulsifier. She felt around the cluttered desk for her hand pump and a moment later, pressed the pump handle until the canister was pressurized. She adjusted the trigger, wishing she'd had time to test the invention, although there was no better way to let a device show its worth than to test it in the field.

While she hoped the man she'd meet at Henry's Leather Works wasn't lying in wait, ready attack her, if he did, she'd find out just how light the trigger pull of her self-defense spray device was.

Anna pulled up her skirt and made use of the secret pockets in her dress once more. She slid the self-defense canister into one and secured the letter from Mister Oppenheimer in the other.

After attempting to untangle the wet knots in her hair with a comb and covering the bodice of her dress with a fresh blouse, she retrieved a dry coat from where it hung on the back of a chair. She pulled the quilted felt on and buttoned up for warmth before collecting her purse and umbrella and hurrying out the door.

With her feet already turned towards 15th and Main, up went the umbrella as she dove back into the driving rain.

On a clear day, the path to Henry's Leather Works would have been a pleasant stroll through the business district. There would be a colorful splash of people, the sounds of commerce, and smells from the many food merchants wafting through the air. But none of those pleasantries existed in this storm. The people rushing from place to place existed in washed out grays, the sounds of life dampened by the incessant prattling of the rain, and the world smelled of must and oil-slicked mud.

Though she knew she'd regret the expense, Anna couldn't fathom walking across town in this weather. Reluctantly, she fished through her purse, finding enough fare to hire a cab. A car pulled to the curb the moment she signaled, and for once she counted herself lucky to live where cabs were plentiful, even when coins weren't.

The cabbie welcomed her aboard and Anna told him where to go. The trip was much shorter than she expected, and she spent every moment watching the poor pedestrians trudging through the darkening rain, thankful that she wasn't among them.

Even with the umbrella, Anna was soaking wet by the time she made the walk from the cab to Harry's Leather Works' front door. The building was broad and windowless, and she gasped with surprise when she opened the door and found the interior decorated more like a bank than a leather works shop. She took three purposeful steps inside and paused to take it all in. The extraordinary interior sent Anna's curiosity running wild.

A woman about Anna's age sat behind a reception desk. She eyed Anna suspiciously.

"Excuse me," Anna said politely as she approached the desk, "I'm here to see Mister Kitchen."

"Mister Kitchen? Not familiar with that one. You sure you got it right?" The receptionist lifted her brow as her eyes trailed down Anna's working-class attire.

"I think so." Anna blushed as the receptionist's heavy gaze dragged across her. She was used to being ignored; an afterthought tucked into the corner of a room. But this woman was taking in every inch of who Anna was and judging her for it. Anna cleared her throat. "I received a letter instructing me to meet Mister Kitchen here. It is an odd name; one I won't forget."

The receptionist flipped perfect auburn curls over her shoulder and rose from her desk. "Sounds forgettable to me. Let me check with the Founder to see if he's here."

Her heels cracked against the tile floor as she approached a large wooden door set into the wall behind her desk. She opened it without knocking and poked her head inside to speak to someone within. A moment later an older man with thick glasses, a fitted suit, and a limp emerged.

"So, you're the one Mister Kitchen is meeting! He doesn't come in often, only for special occasions. He's taking tea now, but I'll let him know you've arrived."

"He knew I was coming?" Anna asked.

"Of course," the man said with a smile. "They always do, you know. Please, make yourself comfortable." He gestured toward a grouping of high-backed leather chairs. When Anna sat in one, she found them far more attractive than they were comfortable.

A grandfather clock standing against a wall chimed the hour. Anna fidgeted, trying to ignore the receptionist who had resumed glaring at her.

The clock had chimed the next hour before the gray-haired Founder finally returned, a pleasant smile dancing below red cheeks. "Sorry for the wait. State business."

Anna was bored, and irritated that she'd been kept waiting so long, but she hid her annoyance behind a patient smile. "It's no bother, I'm sure I can find dinner somewhere on my way home."

"Dinner?" He pulled a pocket watch from his jacket. It was unlike any watch Anna had ever seen; its face glowed brightly beneath its cover, and digital numbers displayed the time with such crisp clarity that when he flicked the watch forward to let its lid fall closed, Anna read the time in the split-second before it clasped shut. "Oh, my", he said. "It's already past seven. Let's take you back to Mister Kitchen."

Anna rose from her chair, stifling the urge to stick her tongue out at the receptionist while she followed the elder gentleman past the front desk and deeper into the building. They passed a dozen dark wooden doors. When her guide finally opened the thirteenth door, it revealed a space larger than Anna's entire flat.

"Anna Joliot-Curie, Sir." The Founder ushered Anna into the room with the announcement and closed the door behind her. Panic rose in her chest when she heard a key turn in the lock.

The room around her ticked and buzzed with the sounds of machinery. The locked door was quickly put out of her mind when a bolt of electricity leapt from a short, slender contraption directly in front of her. She set down her purse and took a step forward, arm instinctively rising toward the device.

"I wouldn't touch that if I were you," a male voice warned from somewhere beyond a screen to her left.

Anna jumped back. "Sorry! It's just that... Is that a Tesla coil?"

"It is." A brawny man in a dark suit emerged from behind the screen. "It's nice to have a visitor who knows what they're looking at. Though really, you should know better than to approach an active Tesla." He reached for a lever and turned the device off. "Most of my visitors don't care about contraptions like this. They're only interested in how much I'm paying to get the job done."

"What do they say when they find out? I'm curious why I'm here. Did the last applicant get cold feet?" Anna eyed her interviewer warily.

"Oh, there's never been another applicant for *this* job. Heavens no. There are only a handful of people in the world with the skills needed for this one." The man smiled, an expression that was more professional than friendly. "Before we go any further, may I ask what your opinions are of the Axis powers?"

Anna folded her arms across her chest. The question was unexpected, and she wondered what kind of test this was. She'd read stories of spies and espionage in the papers; everyone had. There was a blooming distrust among the intellectuals on a global scale as talented and powerful people chose sides. She wondered which side of the divide this man was on. What if he was the enemy?

"The Founder," Anna said, glancing at the barred exit and avoiding the question, "I think he locked the door."

His mouth flattened to a serious line across his square jaw. "He did. It's a requirement of these meetings. We don't want passersby to accidentally intrude. They may get the wrong idea about our conversation."

"It is improper to bring a lady to a room with a strange man and lock the door behind her." Anna said, taking a small step back. Her eyes darted around the room, but there was no window or other door to use for an escape.

"Are you aware of the legal implications of refusing to answer questions from a federal officer?" he countered.

Anna's feet itched to move as her anxiety grew. Suddenly the mechanical wonders in the room loomed large, pressing in on her. The Tesla coil was hazardous enough. What did the other devices do? Were they dangerous? "I may have made a mistake coming here. I don't imagine the people I work for would be pleased with me speaking to someone like you."

"Einstein." He nodded. "I'm sure he'll be very interested to know you were here." He tucked his hands inside his jacket pockets and Anna wondered what he had hidden there. She buried her hands in the folds of her dress. It would only take a moment to retrieve her defensive spray, but a moment may be too long if he already clasped a weapon.

"It's interesting. No one ever tells anyone that they're coming to meet 'Mister Kitchen'. It's the nature of secret meetings. Only the people involved know that they've happened at all." His cheek pinched in a daring dimple, and he tilted his head while he studied her. "Maybe my name has something to do with it. It sounds silly to say, 'I'm off to a secret meeting with Mister Kitchen!' But maybe you did tell someone. A friend? Your roommate perhaps? But you know, I don't think she would believe you, even if you had told her you were coming."

"I do not support the Axis," Anna said, her voice cold as steel. "I won't share my work, or the work of my employer with them."

"Excellent. That makes this easier. It's sometimes difficult to turn over talent that has been loyal to them," he said.

"Turn them over? Like to the police?" Anna's heart fluttered. She wished she had waited to speak to Margaret before following the enticing letter. Silly name or not, this man felt dangerous. If she never returned home, Margaret wouldn't know where she'd gone, or how to look for her.

"No, not to the police." He stretched his hand out in front of him, palm up, then twisted it over so his palm faced the floor. "Flip them. Convince them to help our side instead of helping the Axis powers. It's easier to work with someone already loyal to the Allies."

"What kind of work is this, exactly?" Anna asked.

Mister Kitchen turned on his heel and retreated behind the screen. A scraping sound of wood on stone filled the air, and he emerged dragging a matched pair of chairs. He set them down to face each other, sat in one, and gestured for her to take the other. "Sit," he commanded. Anna's mind tingled with anxiety, but she did as he asked. He slouched casually against his chair's back, crossing one leg over the other. "The United States government is creating a secret device. It will be powerful enough to win the war and change the landscape of the world forever."

"Good, somebody should stop the war. Doctor Einstein is sure it will be a long one. Bloody. But the United States hasn't joined the effort yet, have we? Although we didn't start the war, I suppose it would be poetic for us to finish it." Anna's throat constricted after the words left her. She worried she'd spoken out of turn.

He lifted a curious eyebrow and motioned for her to continue.

"War, in and of itself, is a blight on humanity," Anna said, choosing her words carefully. "The scale of this one, a war across the world more deadly than the Great War, it hardly seems real."

Mister Kitchen nodded, a grim shadow passing over his features. "I assure you, it is very real. But what if I told you this device could end the war without losing a single American soul?"

"What of the enemy's souls?" Anna asked.

"Well, as our enemy, I'm less concerned about them. Isn't that the point of war?" Mister Kitchen's voice was light and flippant. "There will be casualties on their end. But that can't be helped in these matters."

Anna shook her head. All this talk of war and secret devices. Why should he be telling her any of this? "Listen, if you're hoping I'll convince my employer to join your cause,

I'm sorry to disappoint you. I hold no sway in Doctor Einstein's laboratory. I'm little more than a secretary."

"As much as I'd enjoy meeting Einstein, he is too well known for this assignment. If he were to disappear..." he let that word, *disappear*, linger in the air between them. "Too many people would ask questions." Mister Kitchen shook his head, a dark curl dancing across his forehead. He pushed it back absentmindedly.

"We need someone well trained, but not in a position where their absence would be noted. Someone with immense talent, a deep understanding of the sciences, and a history in intellectual circles that gives weight to their presence and sets them apart as a natural leader. But they must also be widely unknown. A woman is perfect for this job, actually. Someone who has worked on the fringes, with connections throughout the scientific community, but who is readily dismissed because of her sex." His tone dropped, changing from business to seduction. "We're specifically looking for the kind of brave, ingenious woman who might invent herself a weapon, hide it discreetly, plotting to protect herself in the off chance she has a confidential meeting with a stranger."

Anna hadn't meant to glance at the folds of her skirt to where the canister was hidden, but when she looked up to find his own eyes trained there, she realized she'd given her secret away. She uttered a note of surprise, and her heart sank.

He nodded, acknowledging the change in her. "We've had eyes on you for some time, Anna. You're clever. I've been to your home and seen your device. Its design is simple, but I'm confident it would be effective. That's exactly the type of initiative that will win this war."

"You can't mean *me*!" Anna's voice cracked. "If you're hoping I'll recruit my mother for you, I regret to inform you that she thinks even less of my opinions than my employer does."

"I have a fondness for Irène, but we have the same problem with her that we do with Einstein. Too high-profile." He looked Anna over from her wild hair to her sensible shoes. "Now you. You have been missing your whole life, haven't you? The dark secret kept locked away in boarding schools and foreign labs while your family traipses across the globe. Very few people even know you exist."

His words pricked at a lifetime of loneliness and lit a defensive fire in her heart. If he were to snatch her away this very instant, how long would it take for anyone to notice she was missing? Days? Weeks?

A phantom of despair sprung up inside her, mocking her for living such an utterly invisible life. She forced the misery back into its well and straightened her spine in feigned confidence. "You know I exist, since you've been snooping around, spying on me. And I'm known well enough to warrant you sending me that letter."

"It's my job to recruit talent to our cause. Though, I must admit that most of the applicants I meet are a bit more daring than you are," he said with casual condescension.

Anna felt her skin flush in response to his belittlement. She drew her shoulders back, straightened her spine, and glared at him. "I hardly think you'll convince me to work for you by insulting me."

He flipped his hand in the air, as if brushing her irritation aside. "You won't be working for me. I'm nothing more than a headhunter."

"Who would my employer be, then?" Anna demanded, patience wearing thin.

"The United States government," Mister Kitchen replied. His tone was dry. Monotone. As if he uttered the phrase a hundred times a day.

Anna scrunched her nose, trying to sort through the absurdity of his answer. "I don't understand why The United

States government would go to all this length to hire a secretary."

He stood, straightened his suit, and pulled a folded sheet of paper from his jacket's interior breast pocket. "They have plenty of secretaries. Hundreds of them, if I had to guess. They're offering you the position of Head of the Humanities Department."

"I don't know what that is," Anna said.

He unfolded the paper, turning it so the presidential seal stamped on the stationery was unmistakable above the handwritten note. He handed it to her. "Nobody does, which is precisely the point. The assignment is top secret, and the person they want to hire is you."

Anna held the paper loosely in her fingertips, as if electricity might spring from it to shock her like the Tesla coil. The handwriting was atrocious, but what she could make of the scrawl matched what Mister Kitchen had told her. "They want me to lead an entire department? That can't be right. I don't have any credentials. I haven't even been accepted to a university for formal study."

"Miss Joliot-Curie, you are the daughter of Irène Curie. Privately tutored, you've shown enough aptitude to work under the wing of Einstein himself. The U.S. government isn't worried about degrees or certificates. What you'd learn in college would be useless. The technologies they're touting in classrooms are decades behind what you'll be working with. You'll be treading in uncharted territory. Creating a product that has never been conceived of before. We'll house you, provide you with a well-stocked lab, any equipment you desire, and staff your department with the brightest minds the Allies can offer."

Anna traced the presidential seal with her fingers. "The U.S. government wants to put a secretary in charge of a secret department staffed by the brightest minds in the world?"

"Not the brightest minds in the *world*. But certainly, the brightest minds on this side of the war. And please, Anna, you aren't just any old secretary, are you?" He leaned down to tie his shoe as he spoke. Anna's gaze was affixed to the letter in her hand.

In a lightning-fast move, he darted forward and grabbed her skirt. Anna cried out with surprise and kicked at him, but he grabbed her leg, twisting it at the ankle until pain radiated up into her hip socket. He groped the fabric of her dress hem with his other hand, and she kicked him with her free leg. Mister Kitchen gripped the chair and with one solid yank, pulled it out from under her.

Anna fell to the tile floor like a bag of bricks, yelping as her tailbone slapped against stone. He flipped her to her stomach and pressed her face to the floor, twisting her arm around her back. She was pinned down, the wind knocked from her, the man's weight pressed into the small of her back.

Mister Kitchen felt around the length of her dress again until he found what he was looking for. As quickly as she'd been subdued, he released her, standing above her with her self-defense invention in hand and a smug look written across his face.

"You are inventive," he mused. She flipped onto her back and pushed herself away from him, panting. He reached a hand to her, seeming to offer assistance, but she wouldn't dare trust the hand that had just attacked her. He returned Anna's scowl with a smile. "Anna, you are an inventor who can create something from nothing. In your experience with your family, and your present work, you understand the politics of innovation. And most importantly, you have the name Curie behind you. That name alone will inspire others to follow you to the ends of the earth. And we need that brand of loyalty to succeed."

"You think I'm some lap dog? Happy to come simply because I've been called?" Anna snarled. "You can't just

She frowned. "You mentioned the weight my name carries. My mother called Doctor Einstein and enlisted me in his service. I'm sure he would have hired someone more capable without her influence."

He nodded, his hair coming loose at the part once more. "Your mother pulls a great deal of sway." He walked behind the screen, returning with a sheaf of x-rays, peeling the first sheet from the pile to hold to the light. Anna's name was scrawled across the top edge. The image was from her childhood when Anna had broken her arm. When they'd gone to the doctor, her mother had decided the equipment he owned wasn't adequate, so she had an X-ray machine shipped to him immediately.

"How did you get those?" Anna asked, her voice betraying her surprise.

"How do we get anything? We ask, and we either receive, or we take what we need. Irène was quite helpful in providing us with your medical records when we were narrowing our list of candidates." He shrugged.

Anna felt her defiance wilt in the face of the ghost of her broken arm on the X-ray film. What did it mean for the government to ask for her medical records, and her mother to hand them over without a fight? She watched him thumb through the film, holding another to the light, a view of the break from another angle. "I can't refuse this offer, can I?"

"You certainly could, but I don't think you will. You're too much of a humanitarian," he said.

"What's that supposed to mean?" she asked.

He stacked the X-rays in a neat pile and handed them to her. "Do you remember how much this broken arm hurt?"

She did. She'd fallen from a tree and the pain was tremendous. Anna had never cried over much, but she cried for three days after that accident. "Yes," she whispered.

"And you're aware of how your grandmother died?" he asked.

Anna's voice remained a whisper. "Aplastic pernicious anemia. A result of radiation poisoning."

"Can you imagine what would happen if the entire nation was awash in radiation? The pain that would come from all those illnesses; uncontrolled bleeding, persistent infections, bones cracking until they dissolve under everyone's skin." he said.

"No one would unleash radiation of that magnitude across a populace," Anna said, though the certainty in her voice faltered.

"The Axis powers would. Or we will. It's simply a matter of who gets there first." Mister Kitchen frowned. "If you want anyone to survive, you will take on this task so when the weapon is unleashed, we have people who can live through it."

Anna pressed her eyes shut and shook her head. "This is insanity. Absolute madness. How can any of this be real?" Her stomach twisted. She had her X-rays, and a letter with a presidential seal. But were they authentic? "How do I know whose side you're on?"

"I thought you'd never ask." Mister Kitchen smiled. He stepped to the wall to their right, lifted his fist, and rapped three times. A panel came undone, revealing a hidden door. A man emerged from the room beyond the opening. He was thin as a rail, and lanky enough that his wrists stretched beneath the sleeves of his worn brown jacket.

"Hello, Anna." The man extended his hand politely, took her hand in his own, and shook it in a gentle greeting.

"I know you!" Anna gasped. She looked from the wiry man with the sharp nose and intelligent eyes to Mister Kitchen. "This is… he is…" she looked back at the man still holding her hand. "Mister Oppenheimer!"

"We met once; do you remember? On a bus in New York. Your mother was giving a lecture, and we joked about how odd it was that you had to buy a ticket in order to see her."

to steady him. "They were primed, not by me; by others who went before me. But I saw the opportunity and seized the day. Heh, heh, heh…" He was wheezing as he walked from the view window to another room in the ship, leaning on the young man's arm.

"Yes, Master," Corso nodded.

Dedic wondered briefly what thoughts passed unspoken in the youth's mind but didn't care enough to ask. And soon it wouldn't matter. "I planned an alien invasion. They all knew it was coming. They all expected it. They had all kinds of high-tech gear ready to combat it. I just preempted the aliens and staged one myself. And it wasn't hard. It wasn't hard at all."

He stopped and turned a piercing stare onto Corso, digging his nails into his arm. Corso froze and looked back at him.

"Do you know?" the old man gritted his teeth as he glared at him. There had been enough cruelty in Corso's training to make him afraid of that look and he quailed before him. "Have you figured out the steps I have not told you?"

Corso shook his head.

"I used their own forces to conquer them," the old man spat out. "And while the invasion was moving across the world, continent by continent, I harvested new recruits from among them. They gave me their freshest resource, their children, and I raised them to be aliens, Corso."

It was unusual for the old man to use his name and Corso blanched.

Dedic stared at him, waiting for a response.

"Yes," he whispered. He had heard the plan many times.

"They became the heroes, you see. That's why they were willing to turn on their own people. Because they believed the lie. They all believed what they wanted to believe, and it was all a fairytale that I didn't write—but I told again and again and again. Until this day. This night, that is."

There were two chairs in the Transfer Lab. Dedic often sat in one and broadcast his mind elsewhere, engaging with his commanders around the world. Corso would stand by and keep watch. This time was different.

"Have a seat, Corso," Dedic said calmly, pointing to his own chair. "It's your turn to celebrate."

"No, thank you," he demurred.

"I insist," Dedic's voice had an edge of steel.

The sheer force of the old man's will pressed on Corso's face, heating it up, tightening his throat, and he found himself sinking into the chair, heart pounding. "Master," he said, "I'm not sure I can do this... I really can't... I don't think..."

Dedic sneered. He had sought out a docile personality in the specimen, though it was something he despised. But he was glad at the same time because it made it much easier to go through with the plan. Any faint misgivings he had were washed away by the wimpy little complaint.

With a grunt, Dedic shoved Corso's head back into the socket that connected him to the transfer framework and locked his body into place. This was the tricky part because he didn't want to find himself stuck once he had transferred into his new chamber. He had to time the locks just right, holding this body in place until the moment when the old body needed to be restrained. He had rehearsed it in his mind many times.

"One, lock him in," he mumbled to himself. "Two, suction his head. Three, climb into the secondary seat. Four, initiate the transfer but *don't rest the head yet*. Five, set locks to close. Six, unlock the other chair..." He was puttering around tapping details into the display and adjusting levers.

"Two and a half... a little celebratory drink..." he said, pouring a shot of whiskey and tapping some powder into it. Stirring it with his finger, he gulped it down, licking his thin lips.

Corso's eyes were wide as he watched him move around. "What are you doing?" he gasped when Dedic leaned over in front of him and loosened his shoelaces.

"Don't worry about it," the old man snapped at him. But he was humming. He wasn't angry at all.

"One, done," Dedic mumbled, "Two, done. Three…" He climbed into the secondary seat across from Corso. He was laughing. "This is beautiful!" Pausing to sneeze, he went on. "Three, done. Four…"

"Don't do it!" Corso cried out.

"So, you do have an idea, do you?" Dedic curled his lip and glared at him with a sideways tilt of his head.

Outside, the sound of marching grew louder and louder. The heroes, shining in white armor could be seen in the distance, filling the street as they marched toward their Conciliator's ship. A faint vibration began and grew as they drew closer.

"They're coming, Corso," Dedic shook his head reprovingly. "No time for whining." He reached out and swiped the panel in front of him. "Four, engaged." The two seats began to hum, and Corso's head was sucked back tightly into the socket. "Five, done," Dedic said as restraining belts tightened around his waist, arms and legs. "Six, engage…" he added.

All the restraints on Corso's body unfastened, but the young man didn't move. His eyes were rolled back into his head.

"Now, Corso…" Dedic, the old man, spoke for the last time in an old man's voice. The marching had grown louder, and the ship was shaking with each pounding step. "Welcome to your destiny."

Dedic let his head fall back and the suction took him into its grip, and the old eyes rolled into the old head. A loud crashing sound coinciding with one of the marching steps reverberated through the room and with a bright flash of blue light, the machine died down.

"Well," Corso's mouth said as he opened his eyes and sat up. "This is nice, very nice."

The old man was moaning and pulling weakly at his restraints.

Corso—actually Dedic now—jumped to his feet with a loud exclamation. "Ha, HA!" he cried out, somewhat absurdly, stretching his arms to the sky, flexing his fingers, relishing the power and youth in his limbs.

The old man opened watery eyes and stared at him in horror, understanding for the first time what his purpose had been. The rejection pierced him. Dedic had never valued anything about him except the body he inhabited... used to inhabit.

The un-Corso swiveled around still stretching and moving in exaggerated gestures and tapped the release button on the old man's chair. He was laughing and humming, dancing clumsily and sweeping his hips side to side. "Oh, yes," he chuckled. "I am God now."

The old man creaked and groaned as he rose to his feet. "Master..." he whispered with a swallow.

"Call me God," the un-Corso said with a malevolent grin, pointing at him for a second before turning away again and continuing his victory dance.

Dedic had been powerful in his aged shell, in spite of all its weakness, by sheer force of will. *What would he be now in a young and healthy body?* The soul of Corso wondered, his breath catching as he straightened in the aged body, and a sharp pain pierced him in the left side. He couldn't bring himself to call the thief 'God'.

"You took me... you took my..." the old man floundered in confusion, unaccustomed to the sluggish brain.

"Oh, Master Dedic!" The un-Corso cried out in mock concern, pressing a hand to his chest. "Are you alright? Are you unwell? I've tried so hard to take care of you as your loyal servant—so hard!" He grinned fiendishly and leaned into him, in his face, so that even a whisper would be loud. "You are too good to me..." The words came out gravelly.

The old man fumbled with his hands, looking for a place to rest them and relieve his shoulders of their weight. Pockets. He found them and thrust them in. The shock began to diminish as fear and anger set in, each fighting for dominance.

"I am Corso," he croaked, twitching his hands in the pockets trying to warm them.

"Master Dedic," the un-Corso replied twisting his face into a semblance of sorrow. "You are rambling again. It's gotten so much worse of late, hasn't it?"

There was something in the old man's pocket. He felt it and puzzled over it, staring off into the distance. Groping it brought a picture to his mind. It was one of the master's many tools for survival.

"I am humbled. No, moved to tears, by your generous, lavish gift to me," the un-Corso was twisting again as if about to break into some more dancing. "Dare I even call you, *Father*?"

The old man glanced at him, bewildered. "What?"

"You chose *me*? *ME*? I had no idea!" The un-Corso tipped his head back and laughed. "I will do you proud, Father, when you are gone..." He swiveled away again, humming and snapping his fingers.

He never expected the old man to attack. Dedic had lived in a weak body for a long time that was no match for younger body's power and had assumed that would be obvious to Corso. When the old man leapt onto his back and wrapped an arm around his neck, he reacted instinctively, flinging his limbs and knocking himself over onto his face.

He didn't know how to fight.

But the old man did and even in an aged body, he was a force to be reckoned with.

The un-Corso yelled in rage and wrestled to throw off his attacker, but not before the plunger in the old man's hand had been slammed into his neck, the needle snapping off under the skin.

"What have you done?" the un-Corso bellowed, scrambling to his feet, and clawing at his neck to scratch the broken needle out.

Elite guards of the Jagged Edge poured in the door, tackling the young man, and pinning him to the floor as he screamed and thrashed, spewing insane orders and demands at them.

"Master!" some of them cried out as they lifted the bruised and bleeding aged man off the floor. "Are you alright?"

"Not him!! ME!!" the younger man hollered, then fell to his knees and started seizing. The guards jumped away from him in disgust.

"He was like a son to me..." the old man wheezed, wiping a tear from his eyes, as two guards lifted him gently and set him in a chair. "I don't understand what happened..."

"Surely, he's not a traitor. He loved you, Master," one of the guards said as the younger man's fits increased, and he thrashed on the floor. "It is some terrible disease, perhaps a final alien weapon unleashed against you in your moment of triumph."

"Perhaps you are right," the old man's eyes gleamed as he looked into the guard's eyes and took a deep, rasping breath. "I fear..." he added, wincing in pain.

"Master," the guard uttered reverently, eyes glistening, wrapping an arm around his frail body as it sagged in the chair.

104

"… it has succeeded…" the old man's eyes lost focus, he sucked in and held a breath, longer than anyone imagined he could hold it, his lips working as if to speak one more time.

"You will rule in my…" the jaw released and wouldn't shape sounds. The breath exhaled and did not return. The eyes' pupils blackened and the body surrendered.

The young man on the floor, gasping for a moment between fits, shrieked and uttered incomprehensible words, eyes fixed on the old man's body.

"He was poisoned," another guard said. "Look." He held up the old man's glass where powder swirled in the dregs.

"Vilar, did he just put you in charge?" a third looked at the one who held the lifeless body, "How in the master's name do you expect to do that?"

The un-Corso writhed on the floor, growling, foaming at the mouth.

"I have no idea," Vilar answered. And turning to glance at the young man that looked like Corso, who was once again seizing, he pulled out a gun and shot him through the head.

"But I'm not doing it alone," he added, spreading his lips in a thin grimace.

The others nodded. They were the General's elite personal guard, the highest tier of the Jagged Edge and the bond between them was strong.

"I guess that makes me Vil-Darad now… Conciliator," the new leader said thoughtfully.

The troops were amassing in the lawns out the window, awaiting the instructions of their deceased God.

"Does anyone know what the next part of the plan was to be?" he added calmly, glancing around the room. Each one sensed the unspoken pact and entered into it without question. Someone else had plotted to take over the world—but they would rule it.

"No one must ever know that this was *not* the plan," Vil-Darad hissed.

"We don't have the codes for the machine," one objected, gesturing toward the console by the seats.

"This hand is still warm," the new Conciliator snarled as he yanked on the old man's arm and pulled it toward the colored glass dome on the console. It lit up when the hand touched it. "Authorize Vilar of the Jagged Edge as Conciliator with full privileges and access," he commanded.

The band around his wrist grew luminous with rolling waves of green and blue light.

"It won't give you everything," someone said.

"It will be enough."

They saluted as he placed his own hand on the dome and began to address the army outside in a victory speech.

"Unnatural Coup" covers the background story for "Cascade", about a Sentinel stationed on earth to protect the people, and "Eclipse" which involves underground human efforts to free the earth.

The Ice Cream Hermit of Ellis Mountain

by Eric Little

I gazed east at the pale fingers of sunrise creeping up over Mount Scott's peak. When you live in the Olympic mountains by yourself, morning comes early. My days are satisfying, the hundred mundane tasks of survival keep me busy enough to not dwell on the past. That's a good thing. I don't miss the cold comfort of humanity.

Out here things are much simpler. I do have friends—the eagle I call Bill cruises by twice a day to check on me. The wolf I named Sam is much shyer, but I catch him watching me sometimes. Wolves are pack creatures, and Sam is a young male out on his own. I think he really misses being part of a pack, and I suspect that I fill a little of that hole in his life, however poorly.

I find this ironic as hell.

I turned my head to watch Bill glide by as he does every day at this time. Then I picked up my load of kindling and made my way back down to my hermitage.

When I was sixteen, I spent some time in the mountains of Michoacán, Mexico. I loved going up to explore the mountain-top ruins of a Carmelite monastery at El Desierto de los Leones with my brothers and sisters. For three hundred years this peaceful community spent part of each year living

107

in small stone hermitages they built by hand. They would follow a vow of silence during the months they spent in the small single-room dwellings. Then the rest of the year they lived together at the monastery and no doubt made up for all that quiet.

Balance in all things, I guess.

I used to sit cross-legged in those ancient, tiny hermitages and imagine what it must have been like to live a quiet life in such a beautiful place. They had a stone shelf to sleep on, directly across from the small fireplace, and I imagined them bundled in layers of hand-woven wool blankets (it gets pretty cold at night when you live at ten thousand feet in elevation), falling asleep three feet from a tiny fire as the wind moaned high in the trees. I had a very good imagination back then. I used to think that was a good thing.

I guess I never really forgot those days, because I ended up here after my world ended, living high in the old-growth forests of the Olympic mountains. After my old life disappeared in a single day, all that remained was a little money, so I had my tax-guy set up an Amazon account that he kept paid out of my accounts. Then I started hiking west in the direction of the ocean. I never made it to the sea, but that's okay. I like it here, and on a good day I can see the Pacific from my hermitage.

Turns out that I really don't need a lot, and everything I can't hunt, fish, or make gets delivered to a post office box in the little town a couple of days walk from here.

Everything except for ice cream.

You need people and civilization for that. I can go months without it but sooner or later I just have to have some of that cold splendor, and this forces me to interact with people to get it. It's usually a little more comfortable than wearing a sandpaper shirt, but not by much.

But the first, long anticipated bite of melting richness makes it all worth it.

The small ice cream shop on Main Street in this tiny summer tourist town is my only real contact with people anymore. Even though the shop girl doesn't know my name, she beamed at me when I finally forced myself to step across the threshold and join humanity for a brief period of both anxiety and pleasure. I didn't even need to order; she always remembers what I like—a scoop of toffee ice cream on top of double chocolate in a dish.

Why did she have to be so nice? I am not a person to ignore such curtesy, so I managed a smile and mumbled "Thanks" as I stuffed a fiver into the tip jar. In my past, I've faced down serious bad guys with more courage, but I think that losing my family like I did broke a part of me.

I politely nodded and she smiled even wider as I made my way to the booth furthest from the door. I sometimes hear a few of the kids I walk past whisper variations on "ice cream mountain-man" and point at me, but I always pretend not to hear. I guess maybe the young ones do recognize my guilty pleasure, but in my opinion, to be named for a weakness is not an honorific. Although kids often see deeper truths than we jaded grownups give them credit for.

The first bite of buttery toffee blended into vanilla creaminess is heaven. When I dug into the rich chocolate for my second spoonful, I shut my eyes in bliss for a moment before opening them again. But all pleasures are transitory in nature, and my bowl was all too soon empty. My spoon made a scraping sound and giggles burst out from the other end of the room. I smiled to myself, then rose to clear my dirty dishes and make my way outside.

A quick stop after-hours at the post office to pick up my shipment of Red Mill flour, Himalayan pink salt, and my new preloaded kindle from an oversized mailbox, then I quickly shed the stink of civilization for the fresh scent of incense cedar and spruce tips. I've built a small camp halfway between town and my cabin, a snug retreat under a stone overhang overlooking a deep valley that is quite comfortable, but I'm always happy to see home the next day.

This morning, I gathered the pine sap I've tapped from nearby trees and mixed it with chopped up moss and rich, black soil. I added a little water and then stuffed the resulting paste in between the exterior stones that make up my forest cabin. It insulates, holds like glue, and within a week, green moss will bloom, eventually covering my stone hermitage's roof in velvet, completely concealing my home from casual sight. The stuff is water resistant too!

I was about to start winterizing my stone hut's roof when the world started bucking and shaking in huge, destructive waves. I bounced on the stone and mud for over a minute before finally coming to rest, bruised, bloody, and shaken. I didn't think I had broken any bones, but my ribs hurt like I'd gone a couple rounds with Donnie Yen, and my head felt like someone smashed a sledgehammer into it a few times, just for fun.

I pushed myself to a sitting position, just in time for the aftershock. The roof underneath me collapsed and dumped me down into the now soggy and smashed single room of my stone cottage. How did everything get so wet? Oh. My water cistern wasn't waterproof anymore, and the entire fifty-five-gallon wine barrel was reduced to three iron bands and a bunch of broken oak planks. Putting my water supply inside where it wouldn't freeze during the winter had seemed like such a great idea at the time. Now all my winter sundries, my dry staples, were flooded and ruined.

"The smokehouse!" I blurted out. I started trying to uncover my front door, but it was blocked with fallen rocks. I looked around.

There *was* a giant hole in the low ceiling, so I started climbing up the collapsed roof. Every time I grasped for a hold it dissolved, but I eventually scrambled up and out.

The world was changed. And not in a good way.

The three grand Sitka firs that lorded over my side of the mountain* are now two. One of the ancients had fallen, sending a number of lesser works of wood to paradise ahead of it as its immense body crashed to earth. A section of mountainside to my left had detached and slid down the tree-filled slope, erasing everything it encountered until it came to a crashing halt where the creek used to pass through. There were several rents in the earth's skin near me, gaping wounds that smell of fresh earth and wet stone.

My smokehouse is intact, thank God. But that's not going to get me through even a mild winter, and this one looks like anything but. I sighed—I'm going to have to go into town and shop, with people crowding all around me. I shuddered, but there was no getting around it. We were only a couple weeks out from the first big snow, so my time was limited, but first I had to accomplish a few things.

It took me the rest of the day to scoop out the water and mud where I used to have a floor and repair my chimney. I was methodical in my work, because if I screwed this up, I could die of carbon monoxide poisoning in the middle of the night without ever awakening. That bothered me, but not because I'm afraid.

When it comes my time to go, I want to look Death in the eye and wrestle him two-out-of-three, despite knowing the Reaper always wins in the end. For me it's not so much when you go, it's how you live your life and go down fighting that matters. This may be an antiquated sentiment these days, but I'm no longer the square block in the square hole kind of guy I used to be. When tragedy strips you naked before the world you learn what really matters. Hard to explain that to someone who hasn't been there.

The next morning, I rose as usual and waved "Hi" to Bill when he dropped by, then got to work restringing the

---

* A reference to my favorite book as a boy.

waterproof canvas over my poor dwelling so the rain didn't get in while I worked on replacing it. Then I grabbed my big saw and headed for the mammoth fallen Sitka. It wasn't easy to get there, the forest floor was filled with broken limbs and fallen trees and the occasional gaping hole in the ground. And virgin forest has never been smooth ground to begin with.

When eventually I got there, I started by sawing two nine-inch-deep channels across the grain of the fallen giant, ten feet across from each other. Next, a "V" cut, then I started the slow gritty work of detaching a bark-covered solid slab of fresh wood large enough to replace my missing ceiling. After installing it I was going to cement a stone layer over everything. This would be a lot more secure the next time we had an earthquake. I try to never make the same mistake twice.

By the next morning, I had a solid roof, and my tiny fireplace was broken in. I tossed back a protein shake and lightly packed my biggest backpack. Then I waved goodbye to Bill and started down my mountain. Sam followed me most of the way.

The cold morning mists welcomed me with a chill kiss as I descended into the primeval forest. It was slow going; only occasional sections of the trail remained. The cold fog dampened sound, but I didn't mind. I'm not afraid of a little silence. The mist felt nice on my skin until the fog dissipated.

At first the subtle sounds of a living forest were subdued, as if scared. I knew that they would come back soon enough. The small creatures of the forest have short-term memory challenges and would soon be chirping and digging their hearts out as before. That's one thing I love about living in the forest. No matter how bad something gets, the forest creatures always bounce back. How can I not do the same? I am a forest creature too.

Usually, I would reach my halfway camp by early afternoon and have time to access the nearby campground's

WIFI. But now it was getting dark, and I couldn't find the stone overhang that shielded my halfway camp. I couldn't even find the ridge it was part of! I dug out my compass since the trail was missing here, and sighted on where the little tourist town should be. Why couldn't I see the electric lights towns are so fond of? Nothing but night out there. I checked unsuccessfully for WIFI connectivity and sighed. I didn't like the feel of this one bit.

That night I bedded down in a hollow tree and fell asleep listening to the ragtime percussion of falling raindrops on the wood over my head. No fire, it was too wet, and besides, some instinct told me not to draw any attention right now.

I woke at dawn and got moving quickly downhill towards the lightless town, wallet in my pocket and my loins girded for battle... I mean shopping.

I kept having to stop and clear the trail, but I always carry a hand axe and collapsible saw with me, so I was able to deal with the problems the earthquakes had left in my path. It was eleven-thirty AM by the time I ghosted into the silent little town.

The smell was terrible. Once experienced, the scent of rotting bodies is unmistakable.

I took a good look around me.

Everyone was dead.

The only sounds were the quarreling of ravens over the choicer morsels of corpses. I froze for a moment, then a long-dormant piece of my mind clicked into control. I studied the dead clinically, moving forward and intently examining the remains of people and animals and buildings, painting a picture in my mind. I was methodical and detached as I slowly waded through bodies of the town that used to be.

It didn't really hit me until I saw the ice-cream shop girl who always smiled at me.

Her crumpled body had been shot twice in the back; she was running away when they got her. An angry grimace had replaced her gentle smile.

Innocents like her didn't deserve to die like that.

I felt a smoldering coal blaze to life in my gut and I knew righteous anger in my heart.

Suddenly I was back in that terrible day, my hand turning the doorknob to my home after returning from a difficult mission. I couldn't stop the memory. I couldn't stop what came next. The fresh-sheared copper of spilled blood greeting me. I had stood rooted in place, unable to understand what I was seeing. My family had been slaughtered like livestock, and the killer had painted the walls with their blood. I started screaming and couldn't stop.

I came back to myself standing over the kind girl's body. It could have been seconds or minutes, I don't know. I shook myself alert and started scanning the little town for the monsters who had descended upon it. My axe was suddenly in my hand. This time it was going to be the murderers screaming.

But there was no one left alive to rescue or punish. I eventually walked down to the river that ran through town to wash my face clean of all this death, but I couldn't scrub it away no matter how hard I tried.

That was when I heard it.

Life.

Somebody was whispering under that upside-down twelve-footer on the pebble beach. Somebody else was whispering back. Survivors.

My world-view shifted. The voices were young. Punishment could wait. I needed to protect the children who hid under the boat. There was no telling when the deadly gang that tore apart this little town would be returning. I had to get them out of there.

114

I jumped to my feet, shedding water droplets in waves as I shook my head. I stepped forward to crouch beside the upside-down hull of a small craft. Then I deliberately scrunched the pebbles at the edge of the boat and waited. The voices ceased.

"The bad guys are gone, but I don't know when they'll be back. My name's Jacob, and we need to get you out of here as quickly as we can," I whispered loudly. It got even quieter.

"We need to go now. How many are you, hiding in there?" I asked.

"Just us three. Are you sure? They didn't find us the first time," somebody very young answered.

"There was a lot happening the first time. Everyone was very excited. Easy to miss things when you're riding an adrenaline high. When they come back, they'll take their time, searching for spoils and captives," I said easily. I know about these things.

I haven't always been a hermit.

"You don't want to be here when they come back," I added.

"We're coming out, don't be tricky and hurt us," the same voice responded.

"Okay," I said, and rocked back on my heels to wait.

I wasn't tricky.

The leader was a young blond girl of maybe eight with an ash-smeared face. A younger darkhaired boy crawled out too, then motioned for the last of them, a very young child of maybe four years. The same age as Zoe had been. I staggered minutely, then settled back and pretended I hadn't reacted. I turned my gaze to the ringleader, the oldest girl.

"Ice-Cream-Man!" she suddenly shrieked and grabbed my leg so tightly there was no doubt I wasn't going anywhere alone for a while.

"Ice-Cream-Mountain-Man!" the boy hollered and threw himself at my other leg. The little one had no idea what was going on, but she screamed happily and latched on too. I looked down in shock at my new appendages, as they shook and cried in relief. I don't know if I've ever been more confused, but mountain men have to be brave, so I awkwardly patted each of them twice.

I hadn't been touched by another human in over two years. Now I had three children reluctant to let me go for even a second. This is *so* not my comfort zone.

But this wasn't about me. Poor kids. Who knew what horrors they'd seen or heard? I tried squatting to bring my head level with theirs and spoke gently.

"We need to go now. Once you're safe I can come back and look for your families," I said, "Let's go!"

It's hard to walk with little people glued to your legs.

Once we got to a good hiding place, I said, "We are going to need more food. I'm going to check out the grocery store. Wait here."

They just held on tighter. I sighed.

Looked like we were all going shopping.

Someone had looted the inhouse pharmacy but ignored the antibiotics and vitamins. I filled a pillowcase, passed it to the oldest girl, and moved deeper into the store. There had been a fire back there, so when I stuffed another bag with cans, I had no idea what they contained because all the labels were burned off. I just hoped it wasn't dog food; it made me gassy.

I found some whole wheat flour that wasn't too damaged, and there was a lot of hard cheese that hadn't turned yet. Hit the beef jerky in the empty beer aisle and filled the rest of my backpack. The looters had ignored the dried beans, but I didn't.

"Time to go. We're headed uphill, high into the mountains to my home where we'll be safe. It's not very big, but it's warm and we have food and books. Once we're settled in, I'll come back and look for your people. Maybe some got away," I said, trying not to let my doubts show.

"Mommy and Daddy didn't get away," the older girl said with a sadness that broke my heart. I looked at the other two.

"I'm Micah. This is my little sister, Ginger. We don't know what happened. Nat saved us and hid us under the boat. There were a lot of bangs and screaming for a while, then it got really quiet. Nat held her hands over our mouths when we heard someone walking by. After that it got even quieter..." he said numbly.

"Come with me," I said gently.

We finally made it into the forest's cool embrace, and I relaxed a little. Not one of the children looked back the whole way. I suspected these weren't the kind of memories anybody wanted to remember their home by.

Later that night we sat peacefully around the fire after dinner. The hollow tree had been too small for four of us, but I remembered a small clearing between two hills. It made a nice, hidden camp.

I guess I have become too used to the company of my own thoughts, because the question out of nowhere surprised me.

"Why are you a mountain man instead of a normal guy who has a real job?" she asked.

She seemed pretty sharp for an eight-year-old, if a little cynical. What should I say? I'm not really used to talking anymore, but I'm not a liar either.

So, the truth.

"My wife and daughter were murdered. After I tracked down the monster that did it, I just started walking in the direction of the Pacific Ocean and stopped when I found a place I liked. I have a quiet life now. How about you? Do you want to talk about... back there?" I answered, my voice a little rusty from disuse.

"Oh—you understand! I'm sorry that happened to you," she said. Then, "Now we're all alone. Please don't send us away," she asked, trying not to show how much that scared her. Her poorly-hidden fear saddened me.

"I'm sorry that this happened to you too. Know that you are not alone anymore. I will never abandon any of you!" I stated quietly, shocked as I realized that I meant every word. What was a solitary mountain man doing taking in three orphans? These days I didn't even particularly like most humans! Did three kids eat a lot? We were definitely going to have to add on to my little hermitage…

About then all three leapt on me, hugging and crying, and I didn't even try to get away.

Not saying I wasn't pretty uncomfortable, but… baby steps. Maybe I'm not really a hermit anymore.

I still miss ice cream, though.

"The Ice Cream Hermit of Ellis Mountain" was first published in the Olympic Peninsula Authors' 2022 Anthology.

Door into the Duck Dimension

By Stephen Hagelin

Monroe Magical Academy

The Basement

Harriet stood with her folded hands in front of her, fidgeting, but not from any sort of anxiety about passing her practicum. She eyed her rival, anxious to perform at least as well as she did. For in all things, magic and make-up, Mary excelled— and she was barely two months older! She gave Harriet a condescending smile, tilting her head back proudly, staring down her pointy nose, her blue eyes flashing, her blond hair perfect, as she patted her black lab, Berlin.

Harriet lifted a hand to toss her dark curls over her shoulder, freeing her brilliantly colored mallard duck, where he was perched and preening conscientiously. Feathers was her familiar, her servant, and assistant, in her pursuits as a fledgling hedgewitch. His webbed foot dangled near her neck, his ample belly spilling over her shoulder, as he pulled a winter feather from his back and tossed it away with a cheerful, soft quack. Mary watched it drift to the ground with a look of distaste.

Their younger classmate, Jose, scrunched his freckled nose as he seemed about to sneeze. He didn't. The child was very proper, and talented, and as he waited for the test to

119

begin, he fished out a bit of dried mango from his pocket and chewed on its end.

"This *basement* needs air conditioning," Feathers commented in a dry hushed quack.

Harriet snickered, but gulped when she received a stern glare from her instructor.

Mary bore the interruption with a deadpan expression, betraying nothing... Jose didn't seem to notice or mind her laughter, as he stared with all the devotion one would expect of a future master wizard, his brown eyes glistening with the precocious piety of the most academic student, gazing up at their... master... Jack Malwitch. But then, he *was* only 9.

What does he even see in this Geriatric Wonder? Harriet thought to herself, scratching Feather's neck absently.

Jack began. "Dimensional magic is the foundational study of all wizards," he proposed, to which they all nodded, more to encourage him to keep talking than from agreement, "for it allows the witch or wizard to summon friendly familiars, or to travel long distances in a hurry."

Harriet rolled her eyes, knowing that he was about to go off on another tangent.

"Why in my student days at Cascadia Community College, I used to eat breakfast at my parents' house in Sultan five minutes before my trigonometry class and then waltz through the Interstitial Space to sneak in through the door while she called attendance!" Feathers burped, but Jack smiled kindly, and brushed a stray hair behind his ear.

"My...uh, a familiar, actually, was one I found by accident on one such excursion, this time heading to Washington State History, when I happened upon a memory of the forests before Bothell became as large as it is today."

"How large is it today?" she whispered to Mary, earning a silencing elbow jab and a choked laugh.

"And in my haste, I tripped and fell headlong into an overgrown fern! Even though I was soon covered in dirt and leaves, and twigs, and… and… pollen, I think, and I heard a strange, small voice! 'Can you get off of me?' it said, and so of course, I stood up and looked in the bushes and in that depression I had created, I saw one of those black and orange caterpillars, the fuzzy ones—a Dreamworm! It was a little flattened but being only the *memory* of a butterfly, it couldn't really be harmed, so it scooched over toward me and looked hard at me with what I think were its eyes."

You're that certain, are you? she marveled, glancing at her watch. *This is going to take the whole class!*

Jack looked off to the side, as if still lost in that dream, clasping his hands together as he continued. "'Do you often go tramping through people's memories?' it demanded. I admitted that I didn't, and that I was on my way to school. But in all this excitement, I was running even later for class, and had gotten lost in that forest. So, I asked for directions, and she didn't want to give them to me."

Why would she, after you sat on her?

"… and so, I picked her up and put her on my shoulder and started backtracking. She grudgingly told me where the exit was and asked to be put down, and well… I was so late already, I forgot to do so, and so I entered my classroom with a Dreamworm on my shoulder and was granted a sharp look from my instructor! I got away with it though, because I used the memories of Bothell's past to describe some of the city's history to my teacher to explain I'd gotten pulled into the reading…"

Mary ground her teeth, her patience obviously used up.

"Dimensional travel is useful in so many inexplicable ways!" he exclaimed at last, taking a few long breaths to recover from his monologue.

Jose raised an eyebrow at him. "Do you still have your familiar, or did she turn into a Dreamfly?"

Jack's brightly lit face fell, and he sighed. "She returned to her dreams the moment she could fly." He deflated further as he said it, his shoulders slumping in relived resignation.

None of this was relevant to their examinations, but then, Harriet wouldn't object to further delays either. She reached up and scratched Feathers' neck, mumbling to herself, "It's a wonder he ever got out of there with an associate of arts..."

Feathers tutted as only a bird could, and said, "Natural studies aside, Harriet, he is still a moderately accomplished wizard, and your instructor. It does no good to belittle him and call him a 'geriatric' has-been or worse. Besides, he's only 35."

35, yes, geriatric, though not in the usual *sense.* Jack worked at a senior home, and on Tuesdays and Thursdays, he taught the local witches and wizards as best he could.

Jose grinned, interrupting gently, "I only just popped in for the test, Mr. Malwitch." Harriet sneered but covered it quickly as Feathers nipped at her earlobe chidingly.

Jack froze, mid-sentence, as he realized the significance of the child's utterance. "A...all...already?" he confirmed awkwardly, as if he couldn't believe his prized pupil was capable of mastering the intricacies of dimensional magic at such a young age.

The boy nodded seriously, shoving his hands in his pockets proudly.

Mary stiffened, but relaxed when her Black Stallion of a dog nuzzled her hand with his nose, and she locked her brilliant, blue, haughty eyes with Harriet's. "Jose is a talented wizard, Mr. Malwitch, that is why he was inducted into our school, isn't that right?"

Harriet bit her tongue. Talent had *nothing* to do with any of this. Malwitch was simply the *only* "qualified" wizard in Snohomish County—the dolt could hardly help himself, much less his students, amount to anything. There was nothing for it though, Harriet's parents still thought he was tutoring her in calculus... fat lot of good that would do, or would have done, for her, but there it was. He "taught" them magic from the glorious auspices of his mother's basement! *Academy* indeed!

"Of course, Mary," Jack said with a self-satisfied smile, as if she'd been complimenting him. "Jose, will you go first?" he asked, bobbing foolishly as he directed their attention toward a mirror-less, once-ornate frame that accented a view of a cobwebbed, concrete foundation wall in tarnished silver scrollwork. Jose seemed to understand what their instructor wanted, but Harriet frowned, and grimaced when Feathers quacked in her ear in a low warning.

"Don't worry," he rasped, in a confident tone, "I can help you cast this door. Did you bring the materials?"

Harriet swallowed, and muttered, "two seagull feathers, an empty snail shell, two cat-eye marbles, um... and... uh..." She produced the articles in her shaking hands, reluctantly handling the last, unmentionable item.

"A slug!" He honked excitedly, loud enough to make her flinch, but not loud enough to alarm her classmates. He snaked his head out of her dark, curly hair, and narrowed his eyes at the boy, who had not obtained a familiar yet. "I am curious to see *his* progress too."

Underlying his tone was the hint that he expected more from her. That was hardly a familiar's job, but in a way, she was grateful, since Jack only occasionally seemed to recognize her presence, let alone her talent. Mary, had secured their teacher's eye; she looked older than her 21 years for one, and she had an intelligent and socially acceptable familiar... No one, no matter how naturalistic, expected someone to have a pet duck—especially one who typically perched on a shoulder, or bore an affronted look when he was taken for a waddle on a leash. Perhaps he recognized her talents because she pretended to listen to him?

Jose snapped his fingers and cast a sprinkle of ashes and grass cuttings at the frame, as a split-second flash of light flicked from his thumb and forefinger, and the thrown items disintegrated into dust. His lips moved silently, and a shimmering light realized itself into the dimensions of the mirror, forming into a spiraling swirl of gray smoke that was shot through with dried leaf flakes, and sparks and embers that wouldn't die out. A hot, arid wind flowed out of the mirror, but the basement was silent.

Jack gulped.

They all stared spellbound and even Jose's eyes widened with wonder, as one of the glowing sparks flew through the mirror, and fell, radiant and warm, to the floor. A pulsing orange light flowed from it, growing dimmer and redder with each second. They all leaned closer to inspect it... a piece of fire, a grain of hot sand that refused to simply go cold. Jose stepped closer and crouched before it, holding his small hand close to test its heat. Despite the shimmering air around it, he tentatively gave it a light pat. But it shrank back like a cat from an icy hand and resolved into a glimmering curled form of low-burning flames.

Jose persisted in touching its back, and slowly pet its fiery coat, from neck to trailing tail, till a warm 'purr' resonated from the Embercat.

Feathers would have whistled, Harriet sensed, but his beak would not permit such a sound, instead he clicked, and bobbed his head as he looked at his own noticeably drab and dirty feathers.

"An Embercat is a rare familiar to obtain, Harriet, but he must give it a name to change its form," he commented hopefully. What he hoped for, she couldn't say.

She rolled her eyes. "Naming *you* did hardly anything."

He kind of shriveled a bit. "A spirit duck is still a duck. An Embercat, well, is still basically a cat. It's just a little on fire," he added with a huff.

Jack observed Jose petting the Embercat with his jaw hanging dumbly open, and even Mary was taken aback. She scratched Berlin's ears muttering a few nervous *who's a good boy*'s out of reflex. Harriet sighed, impressed despite her displeasure with the boy's progress. In a few months, he'd probably overtake Mr. Malwitch and become their tutor... oh, *that'd* be rich.

"You're a pretty nice kitty, aren't you?" Jose asked, coaxing the cat's chin up to be scratched, as its flame-tongue whiskers pricked up and it rose to its feet to arch its back and stretch. It purred loudly, with a hint of the crackle of a fire in its voice.

"Cats can tell who's nice, and who to avoid, kid," the cat replied at last, "you're not so bad."

Jose smiled wide, and picked up the cat, resting it over his shoulder. "I think I'll call you Don," he said, "you want to be my familiar?"

"Hmm..." he purred, "only if you feed me twice a day, brush my coat, and clean up the ash... but what kind of name is Don?"

"Don Quixote," he answered, "a little odd, but an honorable man."

"Hmph," Don sniffed, "that's not bad." He swished his smoke-and-fire tail and the portal to the ember-world faded, vanishing without even leaving a smell.

Jack was stunned. He had watched all this with disbelief, but now he simply was at a loss. Harriet was sure that any more of this kind of shock would render him catatonic—and almost hoped it would. "W... well done, Jose, you've done very well indeed. I will need to instruct you on more advanced topics." He gulped, possibly because he wasn't qualified to instruct anyone in anything more advanced. "Mary, if you please, could you demonstrate for us a dimensional portal?"

"Easily," she simpered, gliding forward in an exaggeratedly "feminine" gait. Berlin, the dog, cantered up after her and sat dutifully in front of the mirror. Mary opened an envelope and cast a sprinkle of glitter, a few strands of hair, and a dash of smoked sea salt at the mirror frame, invoking a few whispered words. Unfortunately, the materials for her casting were not consumed as Jose's had been, but instead seemed to multiply before and behind the frame, as it resolved into a translucent membrane not unlike the skin of a soap bubble, or a watery pudding.

The Embercat snorted or sneezed, and stared daggers at the dog, as fluffs of dander and shed hair floated out of the other side of the portal. Berlin pretended not to notice, but his tail stopped wagging, and he hung his head slightly.

Mary turned and presented her portal with a proud, magician's assistant sort of hand-wave, "This is my room!"

Indeed, Harriet could not have imagined such an overly glamoured bedroom for her rival to have. It was obvious, though she'd tried to hide it, that some assembly had been required. The view through their inter-dimensional window revealed lacy, pastel-colored quilts on a queen-sized bed, with her potion ingredients arrayed on a shelf over a tiny white desk, that carefully displayed her rarely-used alembics, and marble mortar and pestle. There was a magnificent dog bed in the corner, and flowers growing outside her window. Barely visible through it was a view of her neighbors' house, sprinklers were watering the lawn, and a man pushed a lawnmower in the distance. It was horrible. Was she trying to rub it in? Jose's family was pretty poor, Harriet's parents taught music for a pittance, and Jack... well... perhaps he was worst off of all. He observed the scene through the mirror as if he were watching an iconic drama from the fifties: some kind of make-believe idyllic scene of American prosperity before the bursting of their economic and illusory bubble, now observable through the soapy skin on this silver frame.

He shivered and looked away. "Yes, very well done, Mary." He retreated a few steps, rubbing the back of his neck for a minute or so. Harriet stood there, forgotten, watching her tutor with a newfound sense of pity. Not enough to forgive him for being her instructor perhaps, but enough to prick her conscience a little.

Feathers shifted uncomfortably on her shoulder and fluttered down to the base of the mirror. His head snaked around, and he narrowed his eyes at her. "Come along, Harriet," he said softly.

Harriet obeyed, approaching the mirror with the same kind of trepidation that she'd felt when she attempted to summon a familiar—like feeling nauseous but hungry at the same time, with a dry throat, and a hot prickle on her scalp. She reached deep into the pocket of her denim jacket and pulled out the inoffensive items required to create this portal, and then in the opposite pocket, she withdrew the Ziplock bag with the slug, which unfortunately had only grown longer and grosser in the bag. Taking a deep breath, she dumped everything into the bag, shook it up to coat the slug in the feathers, the shell, and the rest, and then turned it inside out and dropped the slug on the ground, with a moist splat.

Feathers stepped over, pecked at it with his beak, tossed it into the air, and caught it, swallowing it whole in a sickening, gagging display. Finally, he sort of coughed, and blew a foul-smelling breath at the mirror, fluffing up his feathers as a tremulous doorway appeared within the imaginary glass.

A soft breezed drifted toward them, and on it the gentle sound of rustling leaves, and the mild ripple of a creek emptying into a pool. They all stared through the initial mist, and then, had varying responses to the sight.

Feathers turned 'round proudly, expanding his wings. Harriet blushed, as she realized just what her duck had summoned. Mary scoffed, and then covered it with a chuckle. Jose was silent, though Don's purr intensified as if he were about to chase down some prey.

Jack let out a sigh. One of those disappointed, yet resigned sort of sighs, the kind a parent gives when their child takes fifth in a six-person footrace or forgets to fill in the circles for their answers on the SATs.

Cheerful quacking carried toward them, and Feathers nearly flew through the mirror to join his family, who were gathered on a tree-shaded pond filled with ducks swimming and diving, or flying, or landing upon its surface. The grass around the banks was thoroughly trampled, muddied, and littered with droppings, and a sickly-sweet smell oozed from the other side.

Harriet snapped her fingers to close the doorway, but nothing happened, so she snapped again, and then again, as she got redder and redder in the face. "Feathers!? What have you done?"

He turned sharply in alarm. "Why I have made this a permanent portal! Aren't you pleased?"

Despite her horror, Harriet *was* impressed. It was just a shame that his permanent portal opened to a duck pond, instead of something useful, like a hot spring, or the gym. Mary burst out laughing uncontrollably, bending over and holding her stomach as Berlin barked in agreement.

The Embercat curled up on top of Jose's head and fell asleep, no longer interested, causing Jose to smile.

Her tutor was silent as he approached the mirror with a childlike, blank expression, and stepped into the Duck Dimension. He found a large rock next to the pond, and plopped down, resting his elbows on his knees, and his chin in his hands. His shoulders sagged, and his eyes grew watery, and he pondered the ducks.

Jose shrugged and left the basement, with Mary leaving soon after. Harriet and Feathers followed Mr. Malwitch through the mirror, standing at a respectful distance.

"Did you bring any breadcrumbs?" Feathers asked, licking his beak.

She shot him a mean look. "You're hungry even after eating that slug?"

He shook his head sagely. "I meant for him." He bobbed his head in the direction of her teacher and set to work cleaning his feathers.

Jack now held his face in his hands, coming to terms with poverty, the ennui of the unaccomplished, and the futility of study, all at once. With a pang of regret for thinking so badly of him, Harriet walked over. Remembering a small pouch of breadcrumbs in her pocket, she withdrew it uncertainly, and held the bag out before him.

She coughed gently, giving it a small shake.

His teary eyes lit on the bag of crumbs like a man facing eviction staring at a wad of cash, and he accepted it without a word. He opened his mouth, and then closed it again, and she had the impression he'd said 'thanks,' but couldn't be sure.

"See you Thursday, Mr. Malwitch." She walked away, biting her lip in thought.

A soft splash announced the first dash of crumbs on the pond. And a quiet, choked sob was swallowed as the first duck devoured the bread.

"If you have some dried maple leaves and pine needles, maybe we could go visit the Dreamfly, and see if she'll come back?" Feathers suggested. "What is a wizard without a familiar?"

Harriett bristled at that, but relaxed, when she glanced back over her shoulder at her teacher again—hollow, and alone. She took a resigned breath and let it out slowly. "Alright, if you think it'll help."

He quacked happily.
"But only because he's no use to us like *that*."
He quacked knowingly.

"Door Into the Duck Dimension" was first published in the *Northwest Independent Writer's Association 2019 Anthology.*

Fault Line

by Suzanne Hagelin

Shadows from the setting sun cast slotted lines across Antonia's face as the platform rose, hitting her with descending strips of color. Her dark eyes glinted orange and blue with each band of light.

It was a desperate plan and though there were several ways it could play out, only one thing mattered.

She was dressed in khaki green hiking gear with utilitarian tools attached to her belt and legs, black boots, and a black cap over her hair. The view of the city expanded and spread as the glass elevator barreled up the Manhattan hi-rise to the hover transport lobby.

"Get me my craft," she commanded as she burst through the doors before they had parted even halfway. She was one of the few people alive who could step into this space and get whatever she asked for without delay. Two androids whipped around and scurried away. Floor tiles lit up with a dull luminescent path to guide her to her vehicle bay and she could hear the warm whir as the hovercar awoke.

The most direct route of escape was to just run for it, without ceremony or guile. There was always the chance that he would underestimate her like he had in the past and let her go, but she was counting on that *not* being the case.

"Stop," Penn's voice called out from somewhere, "Hold the craft."

She was tempted to smile but resisted the impulse. "Belay that order," she insisted with a hint of menace in her voice, increasing her pace.

"Revoke my wife's transport privileges!" the man growled across the distance between them. She could picture his face, eyebrows dropping low over his eyes, nostrils flaring. He might've been considered ruggedly handsome if he cared to control his expressions. In years past, she had found him attractive. Now, he only disgusted her.

"Freeze all attempts to restrain me!" she ordered, raising her voice as she got to the hovercar door. Placing her hand on the panel produced no response. "Come on," she added in a whisper.

"Your privileges have been revoked," the vehicle bay AI informed her.

"*Request denied,*" her husband mocked as the sound of his feet announced his approach, echoing across the bay.

"Challenge the revocation!" she ordered in a voice full of authority—not yelling. That would tip him off.

"Challenge engaged…" the cooperative AI responded.

"Belay that order," the man countered. He was right behind her now.

Antonia rotated around, her eyes narrowing to slits. There he was, glaring at her with that perpetual sneer on his face, wavering between anger and contempt. He slid his gaze down taking in her outfit.

"Getting away from it all?" His mouth spread into a grin, as if he had decided to be charming and reasonable, but his voice lacked even a hint of amusement. "We haven't finished our negotiations yet."

"You have the documents and my lawyers will take care of the rest." She crossed her arms and stuck out her jaw in defiance. "As far as I'm concerned, you have gained the last concession from me you will ever see."

These words came from the depths of her being and were uttered with enough conviction to give pause even to her husband—about to be ex. She could've written them in her own blood and signed them with her last breath.

He hesitated. Maybe she *was* just leaving. She could tell he was scanning her, calculating, adjusting.

The marriage had been much more than a personal conquest on his part. It had been a truce between factions, a merger of massive proportions, a joining of empires. Penn, of the Tandem Collaborative, one of the largest controlling business forces in the world, had maneuvered and practically woven enchantments to gain the Frandelle heiress of the earth's greatest fortune.

Divorce was turning out to be just as complicated.

"Get out of my way, Lazarus," she hissed, "You can't keep me here." She found herself fighting to mask the adrenaline that was flooding her veins and project it as anger.

"Freeze Penn's authority to question my privileges," she barked at the AI that listened attentively.

"Yes, Sir," it complied.

"And restore any other privileges and freedoms of mine that have been tampered with... at *any time* by *anyone*," she added, glaring at Penn, resisting the impulse to put her fists on her hips. He had always ridiculed that pose. She let her arms hang from her shoulders with fingers relaxed instead, and the effort focused and calmed her.

"All privileges and freedoms restored," the AI confirmed.

"Ha!" Penn released a puff of air resembling a laugh. Stepping closer to her, he leaned over into her face, willing her to fall back against the car. "What do I care if you leave?" he added in a gravelly voice. "I will get what I want one way or another, and you don't matter anymore." This wasn't true.

He very much wanted her fortune and she had avoided every tactic he had mounted against her.

And there was something else he wanted more, that he could *never* have.

Antonia kept her ground, gritting her teeth, eyes blazing, heat emanating from her face—pushing back at him with the sheer force of her will. He felt it. He always had. It was the only thing about her he had ever respected.

Her body was twitching with the need to expel all the energy it had collected. And before he could smirk and pull away from her, she punched him in the chest with both fists, shoving him back, taking a step toward him and punching him again.

Taking another step in his direction, she said, "Get. Away. From. Me." She timed each word with the punches and steps, and it had the effect she expected. She needed him angry. Angry enough not to think too clearly. Not to notice.

He grabbed her shoulders and yanked her against himself, catching her in a viselike embrace with one arm, and clutching her jaw with the other. It was a bruising, cruel pinch. "Tanny," he said, grinning coldly, "Don't go there. You don't want to fight me…"

She let him have one moment to gloat, then stepped into the routine she had rehearsed a hundred times. In one fluid motion, she lowered her head, hooked one foot behind his ankle and began to twist, curling and crouching at the same time. As he lost his footing, she anchored hers, planting both feet solidly on the floor, and slammed upward forcefully, jabbing with her hands clasped as if to dive. She broke his hold and before he could regain his balance, clenched her fists and dropped them onto his head, knocking him to the floor. Dropping, she used the momentum to slam him with her elbows, one to his jaw and one to his sternum. It played out flawlessly. Better than she could have hoped for.

134

Then she was on her feet and leaping for the hovercar before he could even roll over.

"You don't know how long I've waited to do that," she muttered as the car door lifted and she climbed into her seat. Her heart was racing. Taking him down *for real* was nothing like she had practiced with her training bot so many times. Penn could be a formidable enemy and she knew what he was capable of. *Not afraid. Not afraid,* she reminded herself over and over as she fumbled with the controls.

Was she really going to get away that easily?

"Wait," he groaned, sitting up awkwardly. "Tanny, you're going to regret that..." He wanted to say more but was finding it difficult to get the words out. For a moment he looked at her with that unsettling gaze that had struck her when they first met. A puzzled, lost, hurt look that pulled on her former self.

Long ago she had loved him. It seemed forever ago.

He rubbed his jaw with one hand and raised the other unsteadily, pointing at her. Did he expect her to feel bad? For an instant she did. Only for an instant... then a gleam of mockery sparked in his eyes and fury rose inside of her to counter it. She grabbed the handle of the door and at the same time, noticed a familiar barrel-shaped tool in his grasp, and heard it click. Something thumped into her shoulder as the door closed and his face lit up in wicked delight.

And he laughed.

Pain spread out through her body like ripples in water. The air was knocked out of her lungs and tears came to her eyes as she fought to breathe, and her limbs trembled. She couldn't utter the commands to leave the vehicle bay. She wouldn't be getting out this way after all. Instead, she hit the dashboard, jerking herself and gurgling in her throat, trying to get the words out.

What was it? What had he shot her with? The fear would make it harder for her body to handle it. *Can't be afraid. Not afraid. I'm not afraid.*

No. She was mad. And that was what she needed. There was still hope.

Penn pulled himself to his feet and came up to the side of the car, leaning onto the window. "You're not going anywhere." As if he had known all along she would run. Her eyelids hung heavily as she watched him, reading his face, wondering what more he had set up to control her besides the tranq.

You're not getting a dime, she was thinking, but hadn't found a way to speak yet.

"I might be persuaded to let you go, though..." He grinned and tapped the window. The AI obediently opened it for him, having no reason not to. Penn leaned on his arms, no longer as muscular as they used to be, but still strong. "You've already given me what I needed most."

Her eyes flashed and she spat at him, an overpowering fear rising in her chest up to her throat. Choking and gasping, she tried to speak. Fumbling with the hovercar's emergency pack, she found and grabbed a water bottle with one hand— the other, on the side where the pellet had hit, hung loosely, unresponsive—and drank, coating and soothing her throat.

"You can't have her," she croaked, referring to their child, the one thing that mattered most in the world.

He smiled with something like gentleness and reached his hand in to pat her shoulder. "Yes, I can," he said. "I already do."

"You have offspring all over the world, I know you do..." her eyes kept watering, but they weren't tears. The drug was coursing through her, numbing and dulling her senses.

"Only one from you... from your genus..."

He was referring to their role among the Keepers of the Generations. For decades, a small group of powerful humans

136

had been running massive breeding programs all over the world, using wealth, jobs, and hardship to herd people together into communities secretly managed by the Keepers. Their goal was to retrieve, or perhaps even create, undamaged, unblemished genetic code. The quality of embryos produced in labs was unable to match the results of actual living communities where intermarriage and reproduction led to select offspring with the desired DNA. Only a few were assigned the status of having attained to the next Gen. The rest remained in their communities and lived their lives.

Each new generation, the numbers of prime candidates diminished, and successful products were exceedingly precious. The merger of Antonia Frandelle and Lazarus Penn had produced only one child and her DNA was the closest to *clean* that had ever been achieved. There were only a handful of children around the world who could be considered her peers. The future of humanity revolved around these purified humans.

At least this was what Penn believed.

He reached in and lifted her left arm, feeling the place where he had shot her. She was sure there must be a dent there, a bruise spreading.

"What difference does that make? Go find another Gen 7 bride and make your experiments with someone else's children. Not mine." She could see a swelling lump on his jaw and it gave her a stab of joy. Do what he will, she would forever know that she had taken him down.

That felt good.

Antonia's eyes started to close, and a faint smile touched the corner of her lips. Another part of her mind screeched in alarm, compelling her to wake and be alert. It was vital that he wouldn't detect the hope she held inside.

She shook her head vehemently mouthing the word 'No'.

"Our girl has qualities no other Gen 8 product has, desirable strengths, fewer weaknesses..." Penn pulled off her hat and ran his fingers through her hair, mimicking affection, knowing it would infuriate her.

"In *spite* of your contribution," Antonia scowled at him leaning away. This gave her a chance to grab the epi-pen from the first aid kit and stab herself in the leg with it.

He yanked it out of her hand as she yelled and began fighting back with both hands. A mad, scrambling and flinging of arms and fists accomplished nothing, so he opened the door and dragged her out of the car. Her legs weren't quite working yet, and she couldn't prevent it. But she managed to grab huge wads of his hair in both hands and pull.

"You'll never have her!" she screamed as every android on the floor raced to their aid.

"Help!" Penn hollered, waving his arms at the droids who obediently rescued him and freed him from his wife. "Hold her!" he added, and they detained her securely.

"Release me!" she ordered, and they let her go.

But then Penn's men were there, and it was all over. Her display of aggression had been squelched. In minutes, they were half carrying her, half marching her, back along the luminescent tiled path to the glass elevator. The sun had now set, and the exterior darkness soaked up light, giving none back.

If he took her back to her rooms in the hotel on the 35th floor, she could rest, sleep, and *hope* she had caused a long enough delay. At the moment, that seemed ideal. Her side ached and her heart was thumping painfully. A sudden migraine had set in and every beat of her heart pounded in her head. She felt nauseous.

Penn was murmuring to his men about her escapade, cursing and glancing at her over his shoulder. It made her wonder if he dared take out his anger on her. She was not without influence.

The elevator went up, not down, farther and farther from street. Gazing out the window, down to the tiny figures swarming under the streetlights like bugs, she sighed. People. Free to roam as they wished.

Penn caught her looking. "You knew I would find out," meaning more than just finding out about her attempt to fly away to a safe haven. She felt sick to her stomach wondering *how much* he had figured out.

"I will never let you have the money," she snapped with a toss of her head that aggravated the pain.

"We'll see about that," Penn grinned. *No*, he knew this wasn't about money. It was about Silvariah. It ached in her gut.

The elevator doors opened onto the penthouse, and his men pushed her forward into the luxurious apartments that had once been her home... even before she had met or fallen for Penn. Before she had found out what kind of a monster he was. By rights it was *hers*, but he had taken possession of it and she let him.

Antonia strode forward heading to the bar, willing her body to be strong and hide the sickness washing over her. She poured herself a drink, knocked it back, and poured another. It would help her overcome the effects of the tranq pellet. The men stayed behind as Penn followed her into the den and closed the door.

The view, over 180° degrees, was breathtaking, filled with the sparkling lights of city buildings and hovercars coasting around below them. They were high above the hover-ways. A waxing half-moon was rising in the east, warm and cream colored, not yet white. So large.

"Enjoying my home?" she tossed the question over her shoulder.

"Our home—my home now," he countered.

"You've gotten more than enough from me," she said as she moved to another corner of the room. "I'm not letting you take anything else."

"That's what we've been figuring out. Be reasonable."

Getting away wasn't the hard part. She had lots of ways to accomplish that. What mattered was escaping with Sil—if she could just keep him distracted a little longer.

"You can't have Sil either," she turned to face him, rubbing her left arm with her right hand, coaxing the feeling back, warming it.

He paused at the change in her manner. The defiance was gone, the fury and fight dissipated. In their place a cold resolve stared back at him. He had enough experience in dealing with desperate humans to recognize unexpected danger but wasn't convinced there was anything she could do to harm him. He cared little for the brief beating she had given him—was almost glad she had done it—though it wouldn't happen again.

"She belongs to me," he challenged, boring into her gaze with calculating hostility.

"What do you mean?" she whispered. Whatever he said or did now had to be convincingly devastating to her. He would gloat and keep his focus on her, not the hour. That was his biggest weakness. It wasn't hard to feign; her whole insides were strung out.

"What happened to you, Tanny?" he put on an air of concern. "We were in this together. You used to believe in what we're fighting for. The responsibility we carry…"

"Not anymore," she said. "Not for a long time…"

"It hasn't been that long. I remember how we used to talk about solving the problems of the world together…" He poured himself a brandy and sat down in a chair.

"Did we?" she cut in. *Stretch out this conversation.* "You had me fooled in those days, before we got married, when I was dumb enough to believe in your words. Perfect DNA would be the answer to everything, curing disease, giving power to those who were noble enough to use it wisely—as if character depended on the genes."

"It does," he raised his eyebrows and shook his head as though agreeing and negating himself at the same time.

"I can't believe I fell for all that..." she shuddered. The effects of both the drug from the pellet and the adrenaline from the epi-pen were fading. That was one of the benefits of her own genetic code, the ability to metabolize just about anything. She would be difficult to poison.

Penn seemed to be recalling her naivete and relishing it for a moment, sipping the brandy. Deceiving her had taken a lot of work, increasing the pleasure of conquest.

"We're a higher level of human," she scoffed, *"above the restraints designed for lesser beings. Our decisions are for their good...* How could I listen to these things without shame?" She started wandering around the room, looking at pictures on the wall, pausing before shelves, moving on.

Penn puffed, not quite a laugh. "Shame is not a part of our circle. We don't need it."

"You..." Antonia accused, gesturing toward him with the hand that held her glass. "You have disgraced even the dreams of our parents, the former Keepers... Clearly shame is beyond your capacity to..."

"I am a higher rank than they are!" he retorted. "We both are. What damaged you? What tainted your purity of mind?"

"Oh!" she jeered, *"that* would be your doing. You are the profane influence that stained me with your... your lies... your fantasies..." She leaned against a bookshelf and stretched an arm out. There had been a sketchpad there in years past. She wondered if it were still there and found herself wanting to see it again.

"They were yours once, too." He emptied his glass.

"No. They weren't." Carelessly, she began searching through the books, driven by a longing for something from long ago, from gentler times before she had been sunk under the shadow of the Keeper doctrine. As if hope lay somewhere in the past.

"We were together. I haven't done all this without you," he said, "I haven't increased our power without your help. You aren't…"

"I *never* thought the same as you. I made the mistake of thinking you were like *me!*" Antonia spat over her shoulder carelessly.

There it was. With a sense of wonder, she pulled the tattered spiral pad out from between two books and opened it to the first page. *Of course*, he had never bothered to declutter these shelves. They were no different than wallpaper to him.

"And now you want out… so you can run from your place in the course of history." He watched her thumbing through the pages of childish drawings.

"Well, like you said," she replied. "You don't need me anymore. You got what you wanted." There. The dreams of a girl captured in colored pencils, full of hope in a different world than the one her parents had painted for her. No projects. No gens. Just people. She had been an innocent child once, like Sil. Was it too much to ask that her daughter have that? She didn't have to be sucked into that darkness, did she?

She let her eyes drift toward the wall of floor to ceiling windows. Was it unreasonable to think she could *change* the course of the Keeper's plans?

"Yes, I did." Penn couldn't care less about the drawings in her hands and was incapable of understanding what they meant to her. But he was watching her intently, deciphering step by step what was transpiring beneath the surface. Reading her. Adjusting. Coordinating his response.

She shoved the pad into a pocket on her thigh.

"Did you think I wouldn't notice what you were doing?" he rose to his feet and poured himself another shot. "You've got a whole plan to take her underground, change her identity, run off and be someone else. I've seen it all."

Antonia's blood turned cold and she held her breath. The chill swept across her face like a ghostly wind. The fear she had been keeping at bay began gnawing at her heart, and a hint of pleading came into her eyes. One finger began to shake, and she slowly pulled it into the palm of her hand, taking a sip of her drink, not daring to look away.

Her plan was evaporating before her eyes. He couldn't have figured it out already, could he?

He saw.

"Passports, genetic cloaks, guides to take you several stations along the way. I haven't found where you intended to end up, but it doesn't matter because the journey will never begin." He watched her, the cat staring at its prey, waiting for it to tiptoe out of safety.

"That's nothing," she said breezily, but her eyes belied the nonchalance. They were too wide, too glassy. "Just to throw you off the scent..."

"Your words are false, and I'm not deceived," he replied, his lip beginning to curl, both with pleasure and disgust. He despised her, even as he gloated over trapping her. "I'm not going to forgive you..."

"You don't know the meaning of the word," she shivered, moving slowly to the windows where the moon continued to rise in the sky. Not high enough yet.

"Our child is the culmination of generations and to lose her would be to lose one fifth of the entire cleansed gene pool! This is a crime against humanity, against ALL races! You *can't* extract her from the project!"

The weight of self-righteousness in his words horrified her. "You have plans for her..."

"My plans are my business."

Antonia leaned her head against the glass, watching her breath leave a foggy circle. Her heart was racing, and she was fighting to keep from hyperventilating. She looked around the edges of the window frame, stroking them with her hand, searching for a latch.

The old-fashioned clock on the wall was ticking. She saw the hand move out of the corner of her eye.

The new identity she had spent so long crafting was real. She had hoped… she had dared to hope that she would be able to use it.

She must not fail. She was escaping but not without Sil!

"Corva Manjer," Penn uttered in scathing disdain. "I suppose you thought I would never look among the Gen 4 projects. A coarse name for an inferior class. You ought to be ashamed of it."

It made her heart ache to hear the scorn in his voice. She had longed for the new name precisely for that reason—because he would hate it so much. "What do you care? Why not just let me go?" She turned her head to look at him, keeping one hand on the window.

"What do *you* care?" he snarled, baring his teeth like an animal. "Why not just let me have what I want?" He flung his hands out and jumped to his feet, leaning toward her with that head, that toothy grimace. "Grovel in the filth for all I care!"

He tossed back the brandy and poured another. "Give up your claims to the girl and I will let you keep half the fortune."

"Half my fortune?" she spoke tonelessly, as though she had no strength left to resist him. "And half of your business empire as well?"

Penn huffed and didn't bother answering.

The moon was growing smaller, brighter, and colder now, sharp white against the dark night. A few wisps of cloud drifted across its face. *It's peaceful out there*, she thought, solidifying her resolve. *One way or another, I am leaving him tonight.*

The hand on the clock inched up to—past—the number she had waited for.

Her hand, still outlining a path around the window frame, found a latch.

Click.

A wild look crossed her face. "Fire. Out the wall," she spoke softly, enunciating he fire escape command code clearly, and the window slid up into the ceiling. A blast of wind burst in, buffeting the curtains and nearby chairs. Her hair whipped around her head.

"What are you doing!" Penn yelled and began jabbering orders to close the window. But she had encoded the commands long ago and he couldn't break them.

Antonia turned around to face him, pouring into her face all the pathos she could, playing out the scene with every ounce of her being.

"If I cannot have her…" she said, looking over his head into the distance behind him.

"What? Are you *crazy*?" he shrieked, taking a step toward her, and grabbing at her arms.

She waved her arms out of his reach and took a step backward, inches from the window, taking hold of one of the bars that framed it.

"Goodbye, Lazarus," she called, tuning the pitch of her voice to the wind.

"Like hell it is," he growled and snagging the strap of her pack, he yanked it off her shoulder. "What have you got in there, a chute?"

Yes, she did. And a few other useful things. All the paraphernalia of a new life, all the things he had suspected and tossed in her face. Here they were, dumping onto the floor as he emptied the pack.

She wasn't surprised it had come to this.

Penn had one of those triumphant smiles that only degenerate humans can produce spreading across his lips and he was chuckling. "You almost had me, Tanny."

He flung the chute and the scattered pieces of her escape out the window over her head. "Not here," he said, "I didn't buy any of that performance of yours…"

She knew he had fallen for it for a moment but now that the game was exposed, he would never admit it.

"Downstairs, when you were running," he leaned toward her letting his jaw hang open in a soundless guffaw. "You had me thinking you were just walking away, and I would see you next week or next month. But this? All this?"

"You idiot," she tried to curl her lip like he did but couldn't hold it. She started to laugh. "You are so predictable!" Six inches from a window with no chute on your back made one a little giddy, even though she knew there was no danger.

His face turned to a grimace etched in stone.

"Did you think I would forget what I've learned about you?" she mocked, "That I wouldn't expect all your devious tricks and snares? I don't have to be cleverer than you! I just have to know you!" She laughed aloud, wildly, carelessly, and he bored into her eyes with a vicious stare, clearly wondering if she had lost her senses.

"You're not going to jump. Come away from the window." He stepped toward her and she stepped back six more inches, toes on the edge, heels hanging over the drop, gripping a bar on each side of the window. The moon beamed through the opening outlining her body with light, casting shadows across her face that the apartment lamps couldn't counter.

Her eyes were blazing with a strange fire and he feared suddenly—not for her, but for himself.

"Lazarus," she lowered her voice into that husky, honey-coated tone he hadn't heard in years. It was unnerving, jarring against his sense of control. "You're not going to get what you want today. Or ever. It's too late for that." And she smiled, taunting, teasing him, reaching out an inviting hand to him. He fought the attraction he felt and hated himself for the weakness.

And he reached out to take her hand even as the realization swept over him. "It's too late," he murmured.

Antonia nodded, sliding her hand up his arm to grasp it tightly, tugging him as though she were unbalanced.

"Sil's gone." His eyes widened and he drifted closer to the window.

She smiled again, twisting her lips just a little in that maddening way he liked. Let Penn scratch at her with his sneers and scorn. She could still irk him.

"I'll find her." He understood now that Antonia had covered the real escape. The child was gone and he had lost his most important asset, and she... she might not react well to what he would do next.

She started laughing again and turned her head to gaze out over the city. Maybe it was time to just step out. The moon beckoned her, and her daughter waited for her, hidden away where this man would not find her.

"Here," Penn said calmly, "Catch."

She whipped her head back around in time to catch him slapping her throat lightly. A tiny nip made her gasp and swipe at it. Something shaped like a mosquito, smashed with a drop of blood, came away on her fingertips.

"What did you do?" she said.

"It's one of those genetic toxins I've been experimenting with. Didn't I tell you about them?" The wind blew his hair around and the moonlight gave him a somber air.

"No, you never tell me about these things. I have to find out through back channels." She glared at him, wiping her hand inside her pocket. *Got to save what I can.*

"You can step away from the ledge now," he said, "and walk out the front door. It doesn't matter. I have the antidote. After a few months when the symptoms kick in, we can meet back at the negotiating table. That's fine with me."

He took hold of her hand, the one grasping his arm. "Friends?" he added incongruently.

They stared at each other. She had Sil, but he had ways to find her. She still had her fortune, but he held her life in his hands. If she fled, she would not survive to raise her daughter.

But if she stayed, it would be worse.

For a moment she considered dragging him out the window, but he yanked himself backwards and grabbed onto the side of the window—so aware of her thoughts it unnerved her. He backed away several steps into the room.

"How long have you had that?" she asked, glancing over her shoulder at the craft that hovered below. It had come when she commanded the window to open.

Penn shrugged. *From the beginning, of course.* As soon as his researchers had figured it out, he had crafted one for her.

There was another identity waiting for her, a better one that, hopefully, he hadn't thought to search for when he found the first one. Should she flee and take her chances? She might find the cure and live. Or would he dare to keep the cure from her if she cooperated? Would he require Sil be returned first?

Minutes ticked by and the moon shifted, rising, shrinking, growing colder and more hostile.

There was the *project*. She had been working on it for months, coding a package that could be uploaded to an AI to protect Sil. It was intended to be a bridge for Antonia to her daughter if Penn separated them. But it was not even close to being finished. If she fled and became ill, would she have enough *mind* left to complete it before death? How could it make up for that?

If he had only been patient, maybe, maybe she would've relented, but it was beyond him. "Do you think I care if you die?" Those words slipped out, tinged with the sour smell of derision. "I have a store of your... fertility. I can make more embryos."

"Do you? Can you?" she countered easily, letting her lips spread into a smirk. He hadn't blocked her access to those resources in time. He had nothing.

He stared at her and she began to laugh again, almost maniacally. It occurred to him that she might jump just to damage her remaining eggs and he dove toward her. Just as suddenly, he panicked at the thought of being thrown out and yanked himself away again in a dizzying fumble, falling to the floor.

"If you jump, even if the jumper-fields kick in... even if you don't fall all the way, the disease will kill you!" He was sprawled on the floor, gripping the tiles with both hands as if the room were tipping and he were about to slide out.

She leaned backwards, hanging one leg down and looked around. There it was, waiting for her.

"Bye, Laz," she said, lowering herself and leveraging down to the outside ledge. Heights had never bothered her like they did him.

"You'll regret it," he snarled.

"I have everything I need and want."

"But you'll die."

"Or I'll find a cure and survive." Only her upper body was visible now, lit by moonlight on one side and streaked with shadow on the other. *Or I'll find a way to hide her and finish the code before my time is up.* She would rather trust Sil to those odds than leave her in Penn's grasp.

"Not in time," he countered.

She shrugged, stretching a leg down for a lower ledge, "I'll take my chances."

"There's a sea cottage in Bermuda," he threw out carelessly.

That was his final arrow, designed to pierce her heart with one last, demoralizing jab, certain he had exposed her greatest secret.

She paused. The lines of tension across her forehead softened, her eyes lightened, and she breathed deeply. Her lips didn't change but her whole countenance began to radiate relief and... triumph. It suffused her skin with a glow.

Penn jolted as if he had been stung. Bermuda had been a decoy.

Then she was gone. He could just make out the sound of her craft as it sped off from the ledge below.

"Damn you, Tanny," he whispered.

The story of Sil, their child, and her struggle to overcome Penn's control and ambitions, is told in the Silvarian Trilogy, beginning with "Body Suit".

Trapeze

By Nia Jean

Luna was lost. Darkness stretched around her, amaranthine shadows and fog, from which she could just make out the shape of trees. A shiver crawled down her spine, as she turned in place in search of a direction to go. Just as she was about to give in to fear, she saw it; a light up ahead. Relief breathed through her body as she took one hesitant step after another, making her way through the dark.

It didn't take long, though she felt damp and cold after pushing through the evergreen branches of the forest around her. It wasn't raining now, but it must have been not too long ago; the boughs were soaked with the evidence. Several times her hair, frizzed up by the moisture, caught on the branches as she pushed her way through them. Drawing nearer to the source of the light, her steps slowed, and bewilderment washed over her. This… was not what she had expected.

Carnival tents, large and colorful, were pitched in a great clearing surrounded by trees. Yellow lights hung in strings, connecting each tent and stage in a tangle of strands, drew her sight inwards toward the center. Had there always been a carnival in the Olympic peninsula? In all the times that she had been to visit her dad out here, she had never seen it. Perhaps she simply couldn't remember passing it on her way.

Curious, she stepped up to the ticket counter and peered inside the stand. A single sign hung on the wall at the back. "Welcome," it read, in bright yellow letters.

Music began to play to her left, and she turned to face an open tent decorated in white and red stripes. Almost without realizing it, she found herself moving towards it, and her steps carried her through the flap into the warm shadows of the tent. Several rows of chairs had been set up, most of them already filled with people, and she chose one near the back and seated herself.

There was a wide circle in the center of the tent with performers doing their acts. Clowns, trained dogs, a seal on a ball. A lean and lanky man, garbed in a checkered purple suit, grabbed her attention. He stood in one place, spinning large hoops in circles and circles, directing them around a young child in the center, no more than ten years of age. Holding a flute to her mouth and closing her eyes, she played a simple melody. "Faster!" cried the man spinning hoops. The flutist picked up her speed.

It was a tune Luna had once known so well that she could have played it backwards. When she was ten, she used to stand in her room and practice with her flute, over and over, wanting so badly to be able to shine when she performed at school. She used to think that if she could only be better, *they* wouldn't fight so much.

The familiarity of the performance left her with a strange feeling at the back of her neck, like an itch that lay under the skin. "I don't need to hear this," Luna whispered. The audience applauded, and she took the opportunity to get up and slip out the back.

She had only taken a few steps when she caught sight of a small crowd of people gathered around a stage. Their gasps of shock and delight piqued her interest, and she found herself making her way over to join them. It took a few tries to elbow her way through the throng, but at last she made her way to the front.

Atop the brightly colored platform stood a magician. He wore a white mask with a glittery, painted mouth, and a triangular-shaped eyebrow on one side. Depending on which way he turned, he would go from looking amused and playful to severe and cold. Sweeping his coattails behind him with a flourish, he presented an empty suitcase laying open upon a table.

It was just like the one she used to have in junior high, that she had covered with baggage claim tickets from her flights to and from her dad's place. The first time she made the trip, she had painted her name with cheap, acrylic purple across its plastic side. L-U-N-A, only the "A" had rubbed off some and looked more like a crooked "I." Her dad nicknamed her Luni-bin because of it. She always liked that. Seeing him only twice a year was hard, but it made every visit special.

A gasp from the crowd startled her from her reverie. With a twist of his hands and a puff of smoke, the magician gestured toward the bag, closed it tight, and began drawing the broken zipper closed. It stuck in the same place hers always had, right beside the handle in the middle. Jiggling it back and forth, he flailed and wrestled with it, the audience laughing at his attempts, before it finally became unstuck. Once the bag was successfully zipped closed, he stepped back with fists raised in victory, bowing as the crowd cheered. He picked up his cane and gave it a twirl in one hand, then brought it down to rap the top of the suitcase. *Tap, tap-tap, tap-tap.*

The sound was so familiar, it reverberated through her as though she had been struck. *Tap, tap-tap, tap-tap.* She had always knocked on her dad's door that way, she would knock first, and he would answer before she set foot inside.

It was their secret knock.

How could they know? Luna thought, her throat feeling tight as she scanned the crowd of people around her. But no matter where she turned, there were no answers for her. Each face seemed blank, featureless, less distinct the more she tried to analyze them. Who were these people? Why couldn't she see them clearly?

"Behold!" the magician cried. The sound of his voice jolted her like an electric shock, and her head snapped back toward the stage. Her eyes were fixed on the suitcase, on the baggage claim stickers and sloppy purple letters covering its surface, as the zipper by itself began to unzip.

At first it was just a hand, stretching out from inside the bag. It searched for the table with artful, exaggerated movements, and pressed flat against it. But soon, more followed. The arm came next, and then the head, revealing a girl with a painted face, dressed in a skin-tight, glittery suit. The contortionist was young, no more than thirteen, her eyes bright as she slithered and crawled, unfolding herself in impossible ways until she was standing upright beside the bag, her face turned skyward.

Tap, tap-tap, tap-tap, the contortionist stretched out her hand, and knocked against the air.

It was only then, after the faceless audience burst into applause, that Luna was able to move again. Hurrying away from the stage, she stared about her with a growing sense of alarm. Something was not right. These were more than just performances, they were glimpses into her past, an unexpected and uncanny breach of her memories. Her mouth opened; her voice too quiet for her words to be heard over the crowd of shadows she no longer believed were people. "I want to leave."

The music changed, shifting from lively carnival music into something more like a radio tune, a popular song she was well familiar with, but didn't much care for. It was just noise, something in the background so that she didn't feel so alone in the car on the way to her dad's place. The long drive through the peninsula was always boring and eerie without music.

Luna's shuddered, her chest painfully constricted. "No," she whispered. "I need to go. He's *waiting* for me."

Legs feeling weak, she pushed her way through the onlookers and staggered away from the stage. She scanned for the exit but saw only tents and more tents around her. It couldn't be far; she had only just entered. Hadn't she?

Luna began to run. She didn't care anymore which direction; it was just a carnival out in the middle of the rainforest. As long as she made it to the edge, she could just walk out.

She scurried around a large tent, glancing over her shoulder, unable to shake the feeling of being watched. Not by the crowd—they were only shadows observing the show, oblivious to her and her fear—but by the performers who followed her wherever she went. They were everywhere. The magician with his mask, the amused side turned as though fixed upon her, following always at the edge of her vision. The flutist sat on top of a nearby tent, her face painted so that it appeared almost porcelain, obscuring her expression. Three clowns juggled schoolbooks back and forth between themselves, one of them laughing, another crying. The third stared right at her, its mask painted to look like her face.

Luna turned down a narrow gap between two tents, her lungs aching in her chest. There was a tear in one side of the larger one to her left, and she dropped down on all fours to crawl inside. It was dark, and music was playing, but no one noticed her as she crawled into a corner and huddled up against the far side of the tent. For a few moments, all she could do was breathe anxiously, trying to calm her racing heart. Her eyes closed, a cacophony of questions swirling in her head.

What was this place? *How did they know?*

A quick-tempod melody began to play from the direction of the stage, once again familiar. It was a piano concerto, her least favorite one. Her ballet teacher always used it for tendu and dégagé, and she could never seem to do them to her teacher's satisfaction. But then, having her mother as her ballet teacher, she could never do anything well enough.

Luna opened her eyes, peering through the stands to watch. Seven heavily costumed performers danced across the stage in leaps and bounds. Despite their sparkling tutus and animated steps, each movement was robotic and sterile. It reminded her of how lifeless she felt each day in her mother's house, flitting from one activity to the next, attempting perfection, and never finding it.

All I wanted was for you to be proud of me, she thought. Tears welled up in her eyes.

Pushing against the ground with both hands, Luna sprang to her feet and raced toward the entrance of the tent. She was desperate to escape before she had to see anymore, and her steps were careless. A stone in the dirt caught her foot, and she fell and landed with a clumsy roll, knocking the wind out of her. For a moment, she thought she could hear the sound of tires, screaming as they gripped and slipped across a wet road, before she picked herself up and kept running. She ignored the ringing in her ears, not wanting to think about what it meant, fighting to force air into her winded lungs. Yet no matter how fast she ran toward the exit, it remained a fixed distance away, pulling ever further back the closer she got to it.

This was a dream. It had to be a dream. It couldn't be real.

Behind her she could hear the sound of the radio, and her mouth tasted like the blueberry energy drink she'd been sipping during the drive. Her steps slowed, a heavy resignation settling over her.

She couldn't outrun this.

Luna turned. Once more she was in a circus tent, a massive one, stretching high above her head and far out in all directions. But this time, she alone was watching.

A spotlight circled around the stage, finally settling on a lone announcer, standing upon a pedestal. His body was crooked, head craned sideways at a shocking angle, and one arm bent the wrong way. He lifted a megaphone to his red and white masked face. "And now," he declared, "The Final Act!"

She could only lift her eyes, following the spotlight as it turned upward to the top of the tent. A trapeze artist, young and vibrant, no more than seventeen years old, raised both her arms in a proud "Y". She smiled, her teeth glinting in the light, cheeks dimpled and head turned just the right way. She always smiled that way because it looked best in photographs.

But Luna didn't have to see the face to know who it was. She already knew.

The trapezist leapt from her perch, her body arching through the air with spectacular grace. With both hands she caught the swing and followed its path to the middle of the tent, only to leap once more to the swing flung towards her from the other side. Back and forth, she cut through the air like she was flying, and the props and stage changed with each trick. Through evergreen trees, looping around mountains, up and down rolling hills. A particularly dazzling flip brought her soaring over the cool dark gray of the Sound.

She stood once more on the precipice before the trapeze, body relaxed as she bent her knees and made the final leap. Her arch across the tent was graceful, but it was wrong. Her eyes were fixed not on the swing, but upon a simple phone she held in one hand.

Too fast, too low, her body began its descent far too soon to reach the rope. By the time her eyes lifted, it was too late.

NO WAY OUT

A frantic cry seized her chest, she made one final grasp at the rope.

Her hand missed its mark, and she fell into darkness.

"Trapeze" was first published in the Northwest Independent Writer's Association 2018 Anthology.

The Last Beer

by Suzanne Hagelin

"Welcome to the ECJF Carnival!" A booming, circus style voice projected in Ray's direction. He had been screened and recognized as a legitimate registrant of the Annual Emerald City Job Fair.

Several people in line behind him hooted, trilled their tongues, or belted out mariachi calls, cheering him on as he stepped successfully through the break in the laser net.

Bells and whistles blasted, colorful lights whirled, and the pink and purple gates dropped into the ground before him. Ray trotted through just in time before it slammed shut with a simulated dungeon door crash and macabre cackling. The chaos in the waiting line outside was nothing to the jamboree within. Jazz music from multiple bands rolled around, melding and vibrating; laughter, like cymbals and drums breaking through the din; costumes that bridged all human history and creativity in a sea of gaudy regalia.

This was the place where everyone gathered to celebrate their job wins and the excitement in the air was tangible and intoxicating. To hear their own propaganda, the ECJF Carnival was a wildly successful event where dreams came true and impossible matches were made. Serfs and imperial-worthy companies faced off in good-natured encounters where all job and employee interview norms were irrelevant.

159

Many people claimed the costume was the key and spent months researching and creating the outfit they believed could get them the job they wanted. One guy he knew had landed a position testing mattresses in orbit, which included regular trips into space, by donning a 1920's gentleman of leisure's smoking robe, slippers, and a monocle. The glass of whiskey and curled mustache were clever, but it was his air of self-indulgence with a hint of arrogant amusement that charmed his employer as he strolled around finding chairs to relax in.

Ray's only attempt at adornment was a black beret with a small green feather added to his usual office garb: slacks and a shirt. No mask or makeup. He hoped to win job offers on merit rather than getup.

Popping in the program-guide contact lenses provided at the door, he scanned the map of the Seattle Center.

"Not the food court!" he murmured, though he would be hungry soon. There were a ton of opportunities for interplanetary food service workers, but he hated the carnival insanity of the food court's jousting tourneys and food fights. And he didn't cook. The dancing arena was a lot of fun but there wasn't a single company there he cared to check out.

"Where would I find off-world opportunities?" he queried the guide in a whisper. A number of events and competitions flashed on the visual, all taking place in the amusement park.

Hmm… CE was running trials at the Spacer, a popular Seattle Center ride that Ray had spent a fair amount of time at in the past. Groups of applicants would be cycling through every twenty minutes trying out for trans-orbit piloting jobs.

The Gravity Hall of Mirrors, built on the site of the old Experience Space Project, was a completely new ride opening that very day. It would be run for the evening by an interplanetary headhunter scoping out candidates for a variety of opportunities.

He scrolled down a ways. "The Drowners' Trap," he vocalized, "Sounds like space vacuum work... Maybe?"

A human whip of party goers swept past him, linking his arm and swirling him into the crowd. He disengaged himself with a chuckle and made his way out of the party toward the rides. Buttered popcorn, cotton candy, and caramel apples filled the air with aromas that made his stomach growl.

"Flinger" was the scariest ride in the center, and he went there first. It seemed like a good place to prove his ability to handle space challenges. The stream of people moved quickly down the line, were sent in, elevated up twenty meters while the harness was attached to their torsos, and then at the top they were flung out across the surroundings in something of a boomerang arc; crazy gees, a gut-wrenching yank, and a tug back to the descent tower. All the rebound momentum was absorbed by the slam-cushion, then a corkscrew slide shunted them back to ground level.

"I'm gonna yell," a guy in front of him announced, "You gotta get their attention." He was wearing all yellow with a black band across his eyes. Ray didn't care much for the banana look but then he hadn't tried at all.

Some people shrieked when they were flung, others wailed. Ray gasped when it was his turn but made no other sound. He tried to pose his body as if he had some measure of control but crumpled miserably at the yank, like a puppet on strings, limbs flailing. And he was unable to recover his poise before the slam and dump down the slide.

Springing to his feet at the bottom, he grinned and looked around on several sides. Robots stood by, ready to invite applicants for interviews. People continued to come down the slide, and several were called, but Ray was ignored.

"Move along, Contestant," a voice admonished him. He had no idea what he should have done or not done, or if it even mattered.

"Was there some…?" He left the question unfinished as robotic cilia on the walls coaxed him to the exit.

Ka-ching! A bell sounded as he went out the swinging door.

You have three job offers in the Seattle Port Authority Warehouse division! The words flashed in his carnival contact lenses. *They have now been added to your carnival portfolio. Return to the PARTY to celebrate or try for bigger wins!*

Consolation jobs for losers. *That's* how they could advertise that everyone goes home a winner.

It's not a big deal, he told himself. Chances are he wouldn't really like a job that expected you to excel at being flung out and snapped back. What kind of work would even need that? For a moment, speculation along those lines distracted him but a current of partiers—obviously with newly awarded jobs—was sweeping him in the direction of another ride.

"Roll and dive! Climb and fall! Show your expertise in the Spacer!" A larger-than-life hologram boomed in the distance, probably someone famous that most fans would recognize, but Ray couldn't quite place him with the flamboyant eye patch.

He found himself picking up speed and clipping around some of the slower walkers, as if getting ahead of them gave him an advantage. It felt good, like cruising in the fast lane past the slower hover cars.

"Only the best can tackle the course and prove themselves worthy!" a beautiful, woman-like robot, glittering in sequins and voluminous folds of velvet, proclaimed in his direction as he pushed through the door. "Are you one of the few?"

"Yes!" he belted out with more confidence than he felt.

She waved an arm draped with fabric and the passageway opened underneath her booted feet. Down he went, into the twinkly sparkle of a starry night, brutally cold, past nebula, burning stars, and light-wreathed black holes, as if floating through space. Soon he was strapping into the spacer car and gripping the wheel.

"Time is of the essence," a deep voice urged. "Find the way and rescue the crew of the Opal transport from certain death by asphyxiation." A bonus game challenge. Low, rhythmic music thrummed in the vehicle walls and vibrated through his body.

Foot poised, eyes wide, Ray squeezed the wheel tightly, waiting, holding his breath. This was good. He had clocked a number of runs on this ride. Then the second the doors pinged open, he pounced, foot slammed into the accelerator, leaning into the dashboard as he shot out.

The maze changed every single day, and no two paths were alike, but there was a familiarity to it that he had learned through practice. Zooming, turning, rolling to the left, accelerating up and over a planet on the right, dropping down into blackness where he knew an opening had to be. Exhilarating, heady, fun. And near the end, in the final stretch, where he knew there was enough room, he executed a flawless forward roll and braked forcefully to zero just before the crash cushion.

The Opal has been found in time and 85% of the crew will live… streamed marquee-style in his contact lenses and he wondered if the percent mattered.

"Forward," a robot instructed as he leapt from the spacer, gesturing to a brown door on his left.

Ray burst through the door as if the aura of the spacer had left a residue, adrenaline still pumping, eyes darting around. *Yes!* He knew his racing put him up there in the rankings. *Ha, ha!*

Over thirty others were in the room, moving slowly and finding places to sit while the hall filled. This was a bit discouraging.

After ten or fifteen minutes and the arrival of a handful more people, the lights dimmed. Ray found himself noticing the costumes in the room as color faded. Not as many sequins or feathers…or faux fur… people were, as a group, less adorned here.

"Congratulations!" A voice broadcast cheerily. "You are in the upper third of the Spacer runners this evening and have been inducted into the minor league pool of potential spaceflight pilot candidates! Well done! These credentials have been added to your portfolio and will open many doors for you!"

Ray's mouth dropped open and a wave of disappointment surged through him. A number of voices around him echoed his sentiment, some cursing, some moaning, some resigned.

The doors that opened *today* led back to the carnival. A scrolling list of inferior, earthside job openings flitted in the column of his contacts. There was a sour, metallic taste in his mouth.

"I should've had a chance," a voice nearby complained. "I was good."

Others were better.

The Drowners' Trap proved to be a frustrating and nerve-wracking ordeal. If wallowing in black water, in a vast tank devoid of light, in a crushingly claustrophobic steel helmet, fumbling with a maze of connectors and tubes, assembling a functioning system that you have to guess at, working with strangers around you that you can't hear or understand—if that's what he had to do to get a job off-world—then he wouldn't.

The exit to that one had a number of vexed faces and murmuring malcontents. No sequins at all. Ray assumed the optimistically decorated folk were too smart to waste their time here.

But the failure galled him. He hated not being able to stand out and it was beginning to feel like his fate this night, wrapping him with seaweed and dragging him down into his own Drowners' Trap.

"I hate it," he mumbled bitterly as underwater construction job ads were inserted like junk mail into his portfolio.

Stopping by several minor stalls, he made his way around the park, not quite gaining the prize in shooting, or snagging the holographic ring toss, or nailing the speed racing on scooter skates—*what jobs would those get you?*—and found himself sinking into a spot on a bench with a tofu dog and chips.

Keep at it or give up and go home? he wondered as he chewed in time to the nearest band playing the latest version of "On Broadway".

"Well, if nothing else," he reminded himself, "Persistence pays off in any field." Somehow, somewhere, there must be a door, or a window.

Not the slammer balls, though... people encased in rubber balls, rolling around bumping into everyone else. The place was filled with aggressive punks and chaos and was just plain stupid.

In the next ten minutes, he was sucked into a 'Bunny Hop' line that pulled him off track a few meters, accosted by two overly friendly androids he was able to escape without offense, presented with offers of wine tasting and fire-walking which he declined, and found himself back on the path to off-world job opportunities again.

By the time he got to the Mystery Mansion he was out of sorts. The carnival wasn't fun anymore.

He was soon standing in the Mystery Mansion game hall with about twenty others of all sizes, shapes, and colors, muttering to himself.

"What's the point?" he complained to no one in particular.

"You're not having a good time?" A guy nearby, looking out of place in jeans and a flannel shirt, quirked a corner of his mouth.

"Am I supposed to be?"

"I don't know. A lot of people are."

A jester nearby laughed suddenly as if to punctuate the fact.

"I don't think they're actually here for the jobs. Maybe they already have jobs they like and are competing for fun. And if they get a good offer, they might take it..." Ray couldn't keep the frustration out of his voice.

The guy in jeans looked at him with a hint of sympathy. "What have you tried for?"

"Spacer, Flinger, a few others." He dropped his chin, staring down at the floor as the lights began flashing around them.

"Looking for off-world jobs?" The guy, lean, hands shoved in his front pockets, seemed well-balanced, as if he wouldn't tip over in a storm.

"Yeah," Ray shrugged and tried to smile. He didn't really care, and it didn't matter. "My earth job just doesn't... whatever... It's fine. I have a paycheck. They like me. I exist and get by." It came out more bitterly than he'd intended, and the strobing red and green flashes made him feel he was being jostled.

"Yeah?" the guy responded, un-jostled. "What would you do if you could?"

Ray stared at him for a moment, searching for the right words. *Anything*, was what he wanted to say, but it wasn't true. He wanted to do something important, find adventure, be involved in something great. And he wanted to have fun while doing it.

The strobing lights swirled faster and the wall in front of them melted away. The mystery had begun and there were puzzles to solve, mazes to negotiate, and spies to identify.

166

Ray hesitated.

The guy waited, gazing into his eyes knowingly and finally nodded. "I get it," he said. "It's hard to put into words. We should get going, though. Some of these are timed."

"Yeah, I enjoy timed tests..." he replied as they shot forward, the guy inches ahead of him.

It was more fun having an acquaintance to compete with, and he made excellent time through the various challenges, even the untimed ones. Never quite putting much distance between the guy and himself in either direction, ahead or behind. The one chance he had, he wasted, when an overly zealous contestant blasted through, knocking them both aside, and the guy in jeans went flat on his back. Ray decided to help him up. It was instinct. Later the hit-and-run character was kicked out for some reason and Ray couldn't resist a moment of gloating. That was also instinct.

They ended up scoring among the top third. Decent... again. Achievements would be noted in their portfolios and *many doors* would open for them... again.

But no one invited them to an interview.

The Gravity Hall of Mirrors awaited, like a beacon of solemnity anchored at the edge of the park. The final challenge, the last opportunity, the true test of mettle. And there were sixty-four prime space positions to fill. Ray felt his heart soaring unreasonably at the sight of it.

He had a chance in that one.

Looking around casually, he realized he'd gotten separated from the guy in jeans and for a moment regretted not asking his name. Maybe if he hadn't started jogging.

"You got this, Ray," he muttered to himself, clenching and unclenching his fists, loosening his shoulders as he loped along.

Entrance to the ride was restricted and whole mobs were being turned away for intoxicants in their bloodstream. Ray experienced a moment of smug delight at the carnival revelry.

Gravity.

Anyone with off-world experience would already have *space-legs*, keeping their head straight, no matter how the sense of up and down changed. For them, the only challenge would be the mirrors. But this was a night for amateurs.

"Do you agree to absolve the Seattle Center, the Planetary Solar Flare Human Assets organization, and the individuals running this event from all liability for any and all…"

Blah. Blah. Blah. *Yes! Yes! Get on with it!* He agreed as soon as the Legal-gram gave him a chance and stepped through the scanner.

He was alone at one end of a hallway, and the place where he stood grew dark while the opposite end glowed like a setting sun, smooth, flowing waves of color wafting toward him… then it began. The first shift pulled him forward gently and grew in strength as the air sped up and what had been a breeze became a torrent. He was ready when the full drop engaged and landed on his feet at the sunny end of the hall, on what had been a side wall.

Mirrors unfolded around him, and he saw multiple, moving images of himself, bathed in orange and red sunlight. He made a few advances before finding an opening and stepped into the next chamber. It began rotating, or maybe it was just the gravity field shifting, and he started to slide. Thousands of reflecting images of his own body, framed in Greek columns, fanned around him. He knew they were optical illusions but somewhere a clue would lead him.

Down was easiest, but not the best way to go. He clawed at the columns and found a real one he could grasp after a few tries. It bore his weight as the chamber continued to roll and left him swinging. He swung back and forth, looking around and decided to fling caution to the wind—*pun intended,* he narrated to himself—and vault himself as high as he could toward some of the mirrors and columns.

Gravity rewarded him with a strong tug just as his feet arched up, before he began to fall, and he found himself in a new chamber with a completely different world.

"Aahh!" he uttered, stunned by the joy and beauty of it all. So much light and structure and sound! Music and ocean waves, the murmuring of voices. He stood and gazed around in amazement as people milled around him. Were they real? Were there thousands or only a few caught in a mirrored chamber that seemed to have no end?

There was a fountain in the middle of the chamber. Ray sat down on the wide edge designed for that and just stared around, fascinated by the canopy overhead of mirrored stars and planets, intersected with clouds and dark blue sky, as if the sun were setting on Earth and the galaxy was spreading across in its place. That one room painted the picture for him. The dream. All fractured in hexagonal reflections on all sides.

"Hey!" the guy in jeans showed up, pausing next to him. "How'd you get here ahead of me?"

"What?" Ray asked, eyes focusing, recognizing him. "Am I?"

"I thought I made good timing."

"Oh," he shrugged, wondering how long he had sat there. "I don't know. I was a little disappointed with the last one, so I got here faster, I guess."

"And sat down for a rest?" the guy grinned, shaking his head a little. "So, you're not trying for the timed thing then?"

"This one isn't timed," Ray smiled back. "I just wanted to relax a minute and get some perspective. It was good."

"Yeah, but you never know what may give you an edge." He sat down as though he agreed, as if he wanted a break, too; as if he wanted to savor the place a little before moving on.

Ray stood up, rocked on his toes, and decided to get moving again.

"Good luck," the guy in jeans said.

"Wait," Ray stopped in mid-turn and looked back. "What's your name?"

"Stan," he answered, stretching out a hand for a firm shake. Solid. Steady.

"Ray," he replied, "I hope you make it out there, Stan."

"You, too."

The rest of the challenge was tough, stretching him, accelerating his heart, revving up his focus, using all his skills and talent. He told himself as he dove over the final bar, pulled his body into a fetal curl, gees shifting, and stretched out to plant his feet and land in a crouch on solid ground—he told himself the experience alone was worth it. He would remember it forever. Dream about it. And he almost believed himself.

But when he walked out into the room and saw the "Top Third" award flashing in his face, it was almost more than he could bear. The most crushing moment of his life.

Good at everything. Top third, in fact, but just not quite good enough to matter.

Exiting the final challenge of the carnival, he almost ran into a bundle of shrieking partiers, all dressed alike in pink, who went running by chattering noisily about their big break into holographic vaudeville.

Ray watched them for a moment. Vaudeville would never be something he cared about, and he couldn't be jealous of their opportunity. But he did envy the thrill of the *win*.

Bitterly.

The door swung open behind him and the guy in jeans came out, eyes on the ground, hands in pockets, not celebrating. He stopped when he noticed Ray's feet and

Eric Little

Eric writes the kind of science fiction he loves to read; world-building with plenty of good action scenes and characters that have a habit of coming alive and not cooperating with his initial plans. He lives on the Olympic Peninsula in Washington surrounded by his beloved rainforest and the sea.

His books include the Good Wolf series: "Bad Dog Good Wolf" and "Bad Cat Good Wolf"; as well as "Summerlight", the first volume of the Summer War Cycle.

Follow him on X (Twitter): @yipman44

Stephen Hagelin

Stephen is an author of epic fantasy books, including the Wingbreaker Saga and the upcoming Arcane Archaeologist series. Most recently he has published "The Lich's Blade," the third Wingbreaker novel. Between working full time, writing, and caring for his child with a chromosome deletion, he is not active on social media.

If you would like to follow his newsletter, please send an email to info@varida.com.

Denise Kawaii

Once upon a time, in the mystical land of Washington State, there lived a reclusive writer named Denise Kawaii who, unbeknownst to her neighbors, possessed an extraordinary gift. She wrote the gateways to realms unknown, all from the comfort of a red Sihoo ergonomic desk chair.

Her books include the dystopian, YA sci-fi "Adaline" series about an AI run cloning program on autopilot.

Find out more: kawaiitimes.com
Instagram: @Kawaii_Times_Author

NO WAY OUT

No way out... No way out... No way out... No way out... No way out... No way out... No way out... No way out... No way out...

Milton Keynes UK
Ingram Content Group UK Ltd.
UKHW050249230324
439834UK00014B/520